Into the M

The girl suddenly reached .... her hands seemed to shoot out of the mirror, into the dorm room.

"Stacy!" Tracy shrieked.

"No!" cried Stacy at the same moment that the girl's hands grabbed her by the shoulders. "Help!" Stacy screamed. She began twisting, pulling at the girl's hands. Tracy ran to the mirror and grabbed for her sister, to try to help her.

She was too late.

While Tracy watched, horrified, the girl gave a final, violent tug, and suddenly Stacy was gone!

Books by Lynn Beach

Available from MINSTREL Books

Phantom Valley™

Stranger in the Mirror

LYNN BEACH

A MINSTREL® BOOK

PUBLISHED BY POCKET BOOKS

New York   London   Toronto   Sydney   Tokyo   Singapore

A MINSTREL PAPERBACK *ORIGINAL*

 A Minstrel Book published by
POCKET BOOKS, a division of Simon & Schuster Inc.
1230 Avenue of the Americas, New York, NY 10020

ISBN: 0-671-75922-1

First Minstrel Books printing April 1992

10 9 8 7 6 5 4 3 2

A MINSTREL BOOK and colophon are registered trademarks of Simon & Schuster Inc.

Printed in the U.S.A.

Stranger in the Mirror

Prologue

Thunk.

One more load of loose dirt fell off the shovel and into the grave.

Thunk, thunk. Another shovelful of earth—and another.

The grave was almost full of dirt now, and it covered the thing that lay at the bottom. Soon it would look like the other two graves, each mounded with earth, each with a wooden cross at its head.

Thunk.

At last the grave was finished. The girl who had been digging set the shovel down, then placed a single flower on the mound of earth.

Goodbye, sister. I warned you not to leave, but you were just like the others. You tried to get away from me. Now you'll stay here—forever.

CHAPTER 1

"**I**'VE never really been able to tell the two of you apart," Aunt Louise said, staring fondly at her twin nieces. Tracy and Stacy James glanced at each other and laughed.

"Everyone says that," said Stacy.

"The main thing is that we know the difference," Tracy added. She slurped the remaining liquid in her ice-cream soda and looked around the Silverbell Emporium, where the three were sitting at a small round table. The Emporium, an ice-cream parlor, was decorated like an Old West bar, with waist-high wooden railings, lariats, steer horns on the walls, and sawdust on the floor.

"Actually," Stacy said, dipping her straw into her own soda, "there are a lot of differences between us. For instance, Tracy's older, by a minute. And I'm taller."

"But only by an eighth of an inch," put in Tracy. "And Stacy gets better grades."

"Because I study harder," said Stacy. "Chilleen Academy is a lot harder than the public school we went to back home."

"But we love it here," Tracy added.

"Don't your teachers and friends have trouble telling you apart?" Aunt Louise asked.

"People who know us *really* well can usually tell the difference," Stacy assured her aunt. "But we do fool the teachers once in a while. We've gotten in trouble for it a couple of times."

The twins burst out laughing. Tracy laughed louder than Stacy, her pale blond hair, pulled back in her usual ponytail, bobbing up and down. Stacy was wearing her hair down. Even so, the girls looked remarkably alike.

"I hope you don't do that too often," said Aunt Louise with a frown.

"We're always pretty careful," Tracy said. "Sometimes we like to fool around, but usually we wear different hairstyles and clothes so people can tell us apart."

"Well, I'm glad to hear that," Aunt Louise said. "Perhaps even I'll learn to tell you apart now that I live here."

"I'm sure you will," said Stacy, who was usually the more serious twin. "And I know you're going to like it here."

"I already do," Aunt Louise said. "The whole area is so beautiful. I've always wanted to live in the West."

4

The girls' aunt Louise had just become librarian at the county historical society in Silverbell. "What I really like about Silverbell is the sense of history about it," she went on. "I can almost imagine that it's the same as it was a hundred and fifty years ago, when pioneers first settled the valley."

"There are a lot of weird stories about Phantom Valley," Tracy told her aunt. "Supposedly, the ghosts of some of the settlers and Native Americans still roam here."

"Really?" Aunt Louise said, intrigued.

"There's an old ruin called Shadow Village that's supposed to be haunted," Stacy said. "Of course, it's just a legend, but odd things have happened there. Animals in Phantom Valley sometimes act really strange. In fact, our friend's seeing-eye dog once got haunted by an evil spirit."

"Really?" Aunt Louise appeared startled.

"Well, *something* weird happened," said Tracy.

"It sounds like a movie," Aunt Louise remarked. "I'm sure I won't regret moving here."

The twins laughed. "There are plenty of things to do and see," Tracy said. "One weekend we'll take you to the pueblo ruins in the cliffs around Canyon Ridge."

"That sounds marvelous," said their aunt. "But what would you like to do today?"

"There's a flea market in the plaza," Tracy said. "That might be fun."

"That sounds perfect!" exclaimed Aunt Louise. "I still need to get some things for my apartment."

The twins and their aunt walked the three blocks down Main Street to the plaza, where merchants had set up booths. The air was filled with delicious smells and the sounds of people laughing and having a good time. It seemed as if half of Phantom Valley had turned out for the flea market. Like the girls, most people were dressed in jeans and T-shirts or long-sleeved cowboy shirts with rolled-up sleeves.

Aunt Louise stopped at a booth that was selling native American pottery and baskets. "How much for this one?" she asked, holding up a small, tan bowl with black and orange swirls painted around the sides.

When the man told her the price, Aunt Louise immediately dug into her purse for her wallet. "This is just what I need to keep by the door for my keys," she told the twins.

They continued to walk through the plaza. At one large booth the proprietor, a very fat, gray-haired woman, sat in a walnut rocker, surrounded by dark, old-fashioned furniture. When Aunt Louise stopped at the booth, the owner immediately spoke up. "Looking for quality furniture?" she said. "I've got some real bargains here. All these pieces come from one of the original families in Phantom Valley."

"These are all very beautiful," Aunt Louise agreed, "but I don't really need furniture, except—well, is that rocker for sale?"

"This?" The woman chuckled. "You want it, you've

got it." She stood up, and Aunt Louise began to examine the rocker more closely. Meanwhile, Stacy and Tracy wandered around the booth, checking out the other things for sale. Some of the pieces of furniture seemed to be more than a century old, but almost everything was in good condition.

"Tracy, look at this!" Stacy said. She was standing in front of a free-standing, full-length mirror. The top of the mirror's oak frame was decorated with carved geometrical shapes. The carvings began on the left side with a large circle stained dark, followed by several crescents, each larger than the last. There was another large circle on the right side, this one lighter than the first.

"Isn't this mirror beautiful?" Stacy asked.

"It really is," Tracy said. "But what are all those carvings?"

"Those are the phases of the moon," said the owner of the booth. "The mirror was supposedly made by an amateur astronomer in the 1830s."

"Wow," Stacy said. "That means it's over a hundred and sixty years old!"

"The mirror part is really dark," said Tracy, staring at it critically.

"That's because it's so old," said the owner. "You could have it resilvered, and it'd be as good as a new mirror."

"I wouldn't do that if it were mine," Stacy said. "I like it the way it is. It makes the reflections sort of dark and mysterious."

"It's really a lovely piece," said Aunt Louise, joining them. "I noticed you don't have a full-length mirror in your room at school, so how would you like it for an early Christmas present?"

"That would be great!" Tracy exclaimed.

Both twins threw their arms around her. "You're the best aunt in the world!" Stacy said. "And I really mean it!"

The mirror was delivered the next day after school. Tracy came back from history, her last class of the day, to find Stacy rubbing the carved wooden frame with an old T-shirt.

"It's so beautiful!" Stacy said again. "And it's perfect in our room! Nobody else in school has anything like it!"

"I know," said Tracy. "It looks as if it belongs here." The girls' room was in one of the oldest wings of the nineteenth-century building. It had low sloping ceilings with beams, wooden paneling, and dormer windows.

"The mirror probably was once in a room just like this," Stacy said, catching Tracy's mood.

"I wonder what life was like here when this mirror was new."

"I've read a lot about pioneer life," Stacy said. "You wouldn't believe how hard people had to work back then. They had to make everything themselves, all their food and clothing."

"I'm glad I didn't live then," Tracy said. "It's hard enough just doing my homework!" She was about to ask Stacy some questions about pioneer life when there was a knock on the door.

Without waiting for a response, Angela Connors pushed the door open and came in as if it were her room. Her usual baggy T-shirt and jeans didn't quite disguise her plump figure, and her short, thick, black hair was poking out from a wide gold headband. "You ready, Stacy?" she asked.

"Hello, Angela," Tracy said.

"Oh, hello, Tracy," Angela said. "What's new?"

"Nothing much," Tracy said, thinking that she wouldn't tell Angela even if she *did* have some news. Angela was known as the biggest blabbermouth at Chilleen.

"Come on," Angela said to Stacy. "We're going to be late for the volleyball game."

"Just a minute," Stacy said. "Look at what just came. A new mirror our aunt Louise bought for us."

"Wow," Angela said. "It's beautiful. Where did you get it?"

"At the flea market in Silverbell," said Stacy. "It supposedly belonged to one of the original pioneer families."

"Which one?" Angela asked. "And why did they sell it?"

Tracy rolled her eyes in disgust. Besides being a blabbermouth, Angela was the nosiest person she'd ever met. *Why is Stacy friends with such a snoop?* she wondered for the hundredth time.

"For goodness sake, Angela," Stacy said, and

laughed. "Who cares why they sold it? It's ours now and we love it."

"I suppose," said Angela. "Anyway, are you ready for volleyball? Everyone's waiting."

"Okay," Stacy said. "Are you coming, Tracy?"

Tracy frowned. "I really ought to study for history, but . . ." She thought about the beautiful grass volleyball court and the fun of the game. "*But,*" she went on, suddenly making up her mind, "I guess I can take an hour off."

"Great!" said Stacy. "I'll help you with history later."

By Thursday night Tracy still hadn't managed to spend much time studying for her weekly history quiz, which was on Friday afternoon. Something always came up. Monday it had been volleyball, Tuesday had been a rented video that everyone watched in the dayroom, and Wednesday she'd had to do all her math homework for the week.

"I'm in trouble," she told Stacy after dinner. "The quiz is tomorrow and I don't know anything!"

Stacy frowned. "Oh, Tracy," she said. "Remember what Mrs. Danita said about academic probation?"

"How can I forget?" Tracy said. Her grades were so poor that she was one step from being put on probation. If that happened, Mrs. Danita, the school headmistress had said, Tracy would have to give up all her activities and would have to stay at school on weekends.

"Don't be so upset," Stacy said. "Come on, I'll help you study."

The girls sat down cross-legged at opposite ends of Stacy's bed. While Tracy closed her eyes and tried to concentrate, Stacy summarized different sections of the history book and then quizzed her sister on them. In the past this method had worked well, but that evening, for some reason, Tracy was having a harder time than usual concentrating. A soft breeze from outside ruffled the white gauzy curtains, and bright moonlight flooded into the room.

"And after Gutenberg invented printing," Stacy was saying, "it became possible for— Are you paying attention?" she asked.

"I'm trying," Tracy said. "But it's so hard. Look how bright the moon is."

"Wow," Stacy said. "And it isn't even full yet."

"I just love it in the West," Tracy went on. "The air's so clear and clean. The night sky never looked like this back home." She got off the bed and opened the curtains all the way. Despite the bright moonlight, Tracy could see the Big Dipper hanging over the pine forest that surrounded the school.

"Oh, my gosh!" said Stacy suddenly.

Tracy turned away from the window. "What?"

"Tracy, look!" Stacy said, jumping up. "In the mirror!"

Tracy turned to the mirror and saw a flash of movement reflected in it. "What was that?" she asked.

"I don't know," said Stacy, "but it seems like it's inside the mirror!"

"What do you mean inside?" Tracy joined her sister in front of the mirror. As she peered into it, she saw that what Stacy had said was true. Instead of seeing her own reflection in the mirror, she saw someone else, someone she didn't recognize—a stranger, a girl in old-fashioned clothes!

CHAPTER 2

"**W**HAT'S that?" cried Tracy, her heart pounding.

"I don't know," replied Stacy. The girls grabbed for each other's hands as they continued to stare into the mirror.

"It's just a picture," Tracy said, trying to act calmer than she felt.

"But what *is* it?" cried Stacy.

"Maybe it isn't really a mirror," Tracy said. "Maybe it's a hologram like at Disney World." She reached out and touched the mirror, her hand shaking.

"Be careful!" warned Stacy.

Tracy jumped back, then touched the mirror again. "It feels completely normal," she said. "There's got to be an explanation."

Together, the girls checked the mirror over, front and back, looking for anything that would explain what they were seeing. It was just an ordinary mirror, though—except that there were moving pictures inside it.

The nearly full moon was shining in, giving a strange silvery glow to the scene taking place inside the mirror. Fascinated, both twins stood and watched. The girl in the mirror was about the twins' age, but had bright red hair caught in two long braids. She was wearing a long-sleeved blue-checked dress covered with a white apron. As the twins watched, the girl bent over a wooden tub and stirred something in it with a paddle.

"What's she doing?" asked Tracy.

"I think she's churning butter," her sister answered. "Remember that butter churn we saw at the county museum?"

"But nobody's used churns for a hundred years!" Tracy said. She studied the scene in the mirror more carefully and realized that everything in it could be at least a hundred years old. Behind the girl was a big fireplace with an open hearth, and just to the girl's side they saw a wooden table with a rolling pin on it.

"It's like a movie," Stacy whispered. "A movie about pioneer life."

"Do you think it is?" said Tracy. "Some kind of movie?"

For a long moment Stacy didn't answer. "I think it's real," she finally said. "I think we're watching a real girl in a real kitchen."

"But how can that be?" protested Tracy. "Where do you think she is? How can we be seeing her?"

"I don't know," Stacy said. "But I don't think she's some*where*. I think she's some*when*."

Now it was Tracy's turn to be silent. "You mean like in the past?" she said. "Do you think this mirror could actually be a window into the past?"

"It must be," said Stacy. "And maybe it's showing us pictures from the lives of the people who owned it before."

"This is too weird," Tracy said. "I wonder who that girl is? I wonder if— Look!" She stopped talking as an older woman walked into the scene. She wore her yellowish-gray hair in a bun at the back of her neck and was dressed in a long black dress. Her face was wrinkled and stern, as if she never smiled. She opened her mouth and began speaking to the girl at the butter churn. The girl raised her head and answered. Now that they could see the girl's face more clearly, the twins saw how pretty she was.

"I wish I could hear what they're saying," Stacy said.

"I wonder what they'll do next," Tracy said.

The girl moved out of the scene for a moment and then returned with a small bowl, which she handed to the woman. The woman stared down into the bowl, frowned, and turned away. The girl watched her, a look of unhappiness on her face.

"The girl looks so sad," said Stacy. "Do you think she's lonely? I wonder if she has any brothers and sisters?"

"This is just like watching TV," Tracy said. "In fact, it's better, because it seems more real." She shivered as a sudden breeze gusted into the room. At the same moment, a cloud moved across the moon, dimming its light.

"Oh, no!" said Stacy. "The picture's fading."

It was true. As the girls watched, the image from inside the mirror began to grow dimmer, and then disappeared altogether. Within a few moments it was once again just an ordinary mirror.

When Tracy awoke the next morning, the first thing she saw was the mirror, and she immediately remembered the strange images of the old-fashioned girl and woman she'd seen inside it. She and Stacy had stayed awake late, discussing what they'd seen and hoping the images would come back. They'd decided that the pictures in the mirror must have something to do with the strange magnetic forces found in Phantom Valley. Homing pigeons often got lost in the area, and airline pilots sometimes reported that their instruments went out when flying over the valley.

"Do you think the pictures in the mirror are really happening?" Tracy had asked her sister just before they fell asleep.

"I'm sure of it," Stacy answered. "That girl seemed so real. I almost felt as if I knew her."

Tracy yawned, stretched and climbed out of bed. Then she remembered her history quiz. Somehow, in all the excitement of the night before, she'd forgotten to finish studying for it. She knew she didn't have a chance of passing.

There was only one answer. She'd have to talk Stacy into taking the quiz for her.

"Absolutely not!" said her twin as soon as Tracy woke her up and explained what she wanted.

"Come on, Stace," Tracy said. "You know it's not my fault that I didn't finish studying last night."

"You had the whole week to study," Stacy said.

"I did my best!" Tracy said. "I'm just not as good at history as you are. You're in the History Honor Society, you'll be able to pass the quiz easily."

"If we get caught, we'll get in big trouble," Stacy pointed out.

"If I flunk the quiz, I'll go on academic probation," Tracy countered. "Besides, we won't get caught. Mr. Taylor couldn't tell us apart. You're not even in his class."

Stacy looked uncomfortable, and Tracy knew she'd won. If Tracy went on probation, the girls wouldn't be able to do any of the things they enjoyed together. No volleyball. No skating. No visiting Silverbell on weekends.

"If I do it," said Stacy reluctantly, "do you promise to work on history extra hard for the rest of the semester?"

"Sure," Tracy said. "Especially if you help me."

"Okay," Stacy said. "You have history last period, right? I have art. All we're doing today is glazing clay pots we made. It should be a snap."

"Great," Tracy said. "And thanks. I'll make it up to you—I promise."

The girls dressed alike, in identical pink denim jumpsuits, so all they'd have to do to switch places was run into a rest room and change their hairstyles.

It wasn't the first time they had switched places, but it was the first time they'd done it for a quiz. Tracy couldn't help feeling guilty. *It doesn't really matter,* she tried to tell herself. *I'll catch up on history later in the semester.*

By the time last period rolled around, Tracy had almost forgotten about the switch, she was so busy. It was the middle of the semester, and all the teachers were pouring on the homework. More important, midterm exams were coming up in the next couple of weeks.

She was on her way out of her English class when her friend Ellen came running up. "Tracy!" she cried. "Come see! The cook's cat just had a litter of kittens."

There were ten minutes till her next class, so Tracy followed Ellen outside to a tool shed beside the barn. There, curled up in a cardboard box, was Missy, the big gray cat, and five fluffy little babies. The girls oohed and aahed for a few minutes, then started back to the annex.

"They're so *cute,*" Ellen said. "I'm coming back to see them right after class."

"Me too," Tracy said.

When they reached the annex, Tracy was about to go to history, then remembered that Stacy was taking the quiz for her.

Her guilty feelings returned when she ducked into

the girls' rest room just as the class bell rang. *Stacy's going to love this*, she thought. *She's never been late for a class in her life.* Tracy was just taking her ponytail down when she saw the door opening. Not wanting to get caught switching, she ducked into a booth and stood on the toilet seat. Tracy waited impatiently while two teachers came in to use the rest room. They were both free that period, and in no hurry as they talked about an educational conference they were going to that weekend.

Will you hurry up? Tracy kept thinking. *Nobody cares about your stupid conference.* Her heart was pounding rapidly.

By the time the teachers finally left, it was fifteen minutes into last period. Tracy combed her hair until it looked like Stacy's. Then she took a deep breath and hurried out the rest room door.

Her footsteps echoed noisily as she quickly made her way down the corridor. She turned a corner—and gasped in shock. Right in front of her was Mr. Taylor, her *history* teacher, talking with another teacher! Terrified, Tracy didn't know which way to turn. She was about to run back down the hall when Mr. Taylor suddenly spotted her.

"Tracy!" he called out.

CHAPTER 3

SPEECHLESS, Tracy stared at Mr. Taylor. How was she going to explain why her sister was in his classroom at that very instant, taking the history quiz? Tracy knew she was in big trouble.

Mr. Taylor took a step closer. "Oops, I'm sorry, Stacy," he said. "For a moment I thought you were Tracy. You and your twin are so much alike."

Tracy continued to smile blankly at her teacher. She was too nervous to speak.

"Don't you have a class, Stacy?" Mr. Taylor asked.

"Uh, well, yes. Art," mumbled Tracy, relieved at her good fortune. She turned and headed down the hall. Once out of Mr. Taylor's sight, she ran directly back to her dorm room.

She was still shaking like a leaf as she caught her breath and glanced at her bedside clock.

It would be too late to go to Stacy's class, she realized. Stacy was never late, never got in trouble. Tracy knew that if she showed up when the period was practically half over, the teacher would guess something was wrong. Besides, she was too nervous to leave her dorm room—who knew what other teachers were lurking in the halls?

I'll go back after school and tell the art teacher Stacy got sick suddenly, she decided. The art class met only twice a week, on Tuesdays and Fridays, and was so large that the teacher didn't always take attendance. Tracy relaxed. It was really no big deal.

"I've got to get organized," Tracy told herself that night after dinner, checking out the huge pile of books and papers on her study table.

"You'll never do it if you keep talking to yourself," said Stacy from across the room. "By the way, aren't you going to ask me about your history quiz?"

"Okay, how was the history quiz?" Tracy asked.

"It was easy." Stacy laughed. "Even you would probably have done okay on it. How was art class?"

For a moment Tracy didn't answer. She suddenly remembered that she hadn't told the art teacher Stacy was sick. *I'll do it on Monday,* she thought. *There's no need to say anything to Stacy, it'll just upset her.* "Art was okay," she finally said.

"Good," said Stacy. "Just don't forget I'm not doing it again, so you'd better start working on your homework."

"Don't worry," Tracy said. She glanced at the mirror

for what seemed like the hundredth time that evening, but there was nothing going on in it. Reluctantly, she opened her history book. "From now on," she said, "it's going to be study city around here."

"I'm glad to hear it," Stacy said.

"Starting later," Tracy added, suddenly shutting her book and getting up from the desk.

"Where are you going?"

"I just remembered I promised Ellen I'd do her nails for her tonight."

"But what about—" Stacy's words were cut off as Tracy banged the door shut behind her.

Why couldn't Tracy take school more seriously? Stacy wondered. If Tracy wasn't careful, she might flunk out of Chilleen, and then they would have to be separated for the first time in their lives.

Jimmy Tolliver, one of the twins' classmates, stuck his head in their room on Monday after dinner. Stacy was alone. "Hi, Stacy," he said. "Here are the U2 tapes you lent me last week. They were great."

"I'm glad you liked them," Stacy said.

"I was going to give them back last Friday," Jimmy went on. "But when you didn't show up for art class, I forgot."

"What?" Stacy suddenly became very cold. "When I didn't show up for art—"

"I thought maybe you were sick," Jimmy said. "A lot of the kids have the flu."

"No, I'm fine," Stacy said, scarcely hearing him.

"Well, thanks again," said Jimmy. "See you later."

For a long time after he left, Stacy just stared at the door. She could hardly believe it. After the chance she had taken for Tracy, her sister hadn't even gone to her art class. Worse, she hadn't told her about it.

Stacy was so angry she was shaking. She slammed her English book shut as Tracy barged into the room, breathless from running.

"Hi, Stace," she said, then stopped when she saw the angry expression on her sister's face. "What's wrong?"

"What's wrong?" Stacy echoed. "What's wrong? I risked getting suspended to take your history quiz on Friday, and you didn't even show up for my art class!"

"Uh-oh," Tracy said, suddenly looking upset.

"Is that all you can say, 'Uh-oh'? The least you could have done was tell me about it!" Stacy was so angry she was shouting, so she forced herself to calm down. "I suppose you have a good reason," she went on.

"It got too late to go," said Tracy. "And I'm really sorry, Stace. I was going to tell the teacher you were sick, but I forgot. I'll tell her tomorrow that I forgot on Friday. I'll tell her it was my fault, I promise."

"Oh, that's going to help a lot," Stacy said.

"Really," Tracy went on. "Everybody in school is sick anyway. I know your teacher will believe me. No big deal."

"It's no big deal to you," said Stacy bitterly. "You're *used* to getting in trouble."

"I said I was sorry," Tracy said. "And I promise

23

I'll— Oh, my gosh!" Tracy was facing the mirror, her eyes suddenly wide with surprise.

Quickly Stacy turned to see what Tracy was staring at. Inside the mirror, the woman and the girl were sitting at the table, talking. But what made the scene most astonishing was that, despite the full moon shining in the window, the colors were as bright and vivid as those in real life.

"It looks like it's happening right in this room," Tracy whispered.

"I wonder why?" Stacy said. "Maybe the effect, whatever it is, gets stronger as time goes on."

Their quarrel forgotten for a minute, the girls began to watch, instantly absorbed in the world inside the mirror. While the old woman knitted, the girl shelled peas into a ceramic bowl on her lap. As she worked she talked, a sad expression on her face. The woman nodded from time to time. After a moment the woman stood and moved out of the picture.

"I wonder where she went?" Tracy said. "I wonder what the rest of their house is like?"

"There's no way to know," said Stacy. "I wish there was some way we could talk to them, or—" She stopped, and just as suddenly, the girl in the mirror stopped shelling peas and stared directly into the mirror.

"Do you see that?" shrieked Tracy. "She's looking right at us!"

"She seems to be, yes," Stacy said, wonder in her voice. She half stood. At the same moment, the girl rose from her seat at the table. It was almost as if they were reflections of each other.

While Tracy watched, fascinated, her sister and the girl slowly approached the mirror from opposite sides. Stacy's eyes were wide open, but she seemed to be in a trance. Moving just as slowly, the girl in the mirror raised her hand to wave Stacy nearer. Stacy moved closer to the mirror.

Suddenly the girl reached forward. Her hands seemed to shoot out of the mirror, into the dorm room.

"Stacy!" Tracy shrieked.

"No!" cried Stacy at the same moment that the girl's hands grabbed her by the shoulders. "Help!" Stacy screamed. She began twisting, pulling at the girl's hands. Tracy ran to the mirror and grabbed for her sister, to try to help her.

She was too late.

While Tracy watched horrified, the red-haired girl gave a final, violent tug, and Stacy was gone! She had been pulled inside the smooth glass surface of the mirror.

CHAPTER 4

TRACY

"**N**O!" Tracy cried out in horror, not believing what she had just seen. "Stacy! Stacy!"

One second her sister was there, reaching for the mirror, and the next she was gone.

Tracy reached out to touch the smooth, cool surface of the mirror. "Stacy!" she called again. She peered into the mirror's shiny depths, but there was no sign of her twin or of the scene that had been there just moments before. Only her own, shocked image was reflected back at her. Fighting tears, Tracy grabbed the edge of the mirror and began to shake it, still calling Stacy's name.

"This is impossible!" she cried out loud. She moved around behind the heavy mirror and checked there. There was no sign of Stacy.

I'm dreaming, she thought. *This is all a terrible nightmare. Any minute now I'll wake up.*

Or maybe it's all a joke, she thought wildly. *Maybe Stacy's trying to get back at me because I don't study enough.* "Stacy?" she called. "Please come back. Please. I promise I'll study harder."

She got down on her knees and checked under her sister's bed. The elastic holding her ponytail snapped and she pulled it out. She couldn't be bothered putting her hair back up as she searched the tiny closet. It was no use, she realized after several minutes of searching—Stacy was gone. She was in the world behind the mirror.

Tracy knew that what had just happened was impossible. She also knew it was true. She sat on Stacy's bed and forced herself to breathe slowly, to calm down and try to think clearly. It was no use—she couldn't think at all. Her hands were shaking and her chest was so tight she could barely breathe. *I've got to get help,* she realized. *I'll get Mrs. Danita. She'll know what to do.*

She had started to stand up when there was a sharp rapping at the door. Before she could ask who it was, the door opened and there stood Mrs. Danita, looking angry and upset. "Good evening, Stacy," she said.

"Oh, Mrs. Danita," Tracy said, trying to keep the tears out of her voice, "I was just going to come see you."

"I'm glad to hear it," Mrs. Danita said. "I hope you were coming to explain why you were absent from art class last Friday. It's not like you to cut class."

Tracy just stared at Mrs. Danita, not understanding her. Slowly she realized that the headmistress was talking about what had happened last Friday. It seemed like ten years ago.

"I just found out about it," Mrs. Danita went on. "I was away all weekend."

Suddenly Tracy realized that Mrs. Danita thought she was Stacy because her hair was down.

"You know the rules," Mrs. Danita continued. "Skipping class results in automatic probation for one month. But because you're such a good student, I thought I'd give you a chance to explain before I applied the penalty."

Now that Tracy understood what was going on, she knew she had to protect Stacy. There was only one way she could think of. "I'm sorry," she told Mrs. Danita. "I was sick. I got sick during fifth period and came to my room. Tracy was supposed to tell the teacher but she forgot."

"Oh, dear," Mrs. Danita said, her expression changing to one of sympathy. Now she looked more closely at Tracy. "You do look a little flushed," she said. "Are you still feeling ill?"

"I just figured it was a cold," Tracy said, thinking quickly. "I went to class today, but now I feel much worse. Maybe I have the flu like everybody else."

"Well, you should have made sure the art teacher was informed," Mrs. Danita said. "I do realize you can't be held responsible for your sister, though."

"Does that mean you won't put me on probation?" Tracy asked.

"I'm satisfied with your explanation, yes," Mrs. Danita answered. "But if anything like this happens in the future, see to it that you go to the nurse or to me."

Tracy nodded.

"Just get into bed and rest now," she went on. "And promise me you'll see the nurse in the morning."

"I promise," Tracy said. "Thank you."

As soon as Mrs. Danita left, Tracy went to the mirror, hoping that she'd find Stacy in it. All it showed was her own frightened-looking face.

What am I going to do now? she asked herself. She realized that she couldn't tell Mrs. Danita what had happened to Stacy. Not after she'd just pretended to be Stacy. If she said anything, Mrs. Danita would probably figure out that Stacy had taken her test for her.

Besides, why would Mrs. Danita believe that anyone could disappear into a mirror? Tracy knew she wouldn't have believed it herself if she hadn't seen it happen.

I've got to find a way to get her back myself, Tracy finally decided. But how? How could she get her sister back from inside a mirror? She sat on the end of Stacy's bed and stared at the mirror, thinking.

If Stacy was able to go into the mirror, she told herself, then there had to be a way for her to come out. Until Stacy found the way, though, Tracy was going to have to pretend that her sister was still here at Chilleen and attending classes. Somehow, she was going to have to be both herself *and* Stacy until she found a way to save her sister.

And she was going to have to do it without anyone suspecting that anything was wrong.

CHAPTER 5

STACY

*A*S Stacy felt herself being pulled into the mirror, her body began to tingle. Then she felt herself growing light-headed and dizzy. The next thing she knew, she was standing in a house that was at once exotic and familiar. Beneath her feet were rough-cut, wide boards, while in front of her stood a huge soot-blackened fireplace. To one side of it was a long table covered with a checkered tablecloth; on the other side, a long, uncomfortable-looking sofa. The room was dimly illuminated by flickering candles and a kerosene lamp.

Still a little dizzy, she glanced around the room in confusion. "Where . . . ?" she said. "What . . . ?"

In answer, someone gripped her hand and gave it a squeeze.

"You've come!" exclaimed a girl, her voice sweet. "You've come, just as I knew you would." The hand tugged on Stacy's and turned her around.

She found herself facing a mirror that was just like the one in her room. Only this mirror looked new, its glass shiny and clear. Standing beside the mirror was the red-haired girl she had seen in her mirror at Chilleen.

The girl was smiling as if her dearest wish had just come true. "I've been wishing for you for a long time," she said. "I knew you would come."

Stacy stared at the girl, confused. "Who are you?" she asked.

"My name is Philomena," the girl said. "I live here, and now you do too. What is your name?"

"I'm Stacy . . . Stacy James. But I don't live here at all," Stacy explained. "I live at the Chilleen Academy."

"I have heard the name Chilleen," the girl said. "I believe it belongs to a family in the valley. Are you related to them?"

"No," said Stacy. *What a strange dream,* she thought. *And it seems so real!*

"We're going to have such a happy time together," Philomena said. Her face was sweet and loving, and she looked younger than she had in the mirror.

"This is such a strange dream," Stacy said.

"A dream?" said Philomena. "You believe you are dreaming?"

"Of course," Stacy said. "I must be."

Philomena's face changed suddenly, the sweet expression replaced by a scowl. Moving quickly, she leaned forward and pinched Stacy's cheek, *hard*. "Did that feel like a dream?" she asked.

Stacy jumped back, shocked. The pinch had been real and it hurt. Her heart thudding in fright, Stacy knew for certain that she wasn't dreaming, that she had really come through the mirror. She looked in horror at Philomena, who was once again smiling sweetly.

"I'm sorry," Philomena said, her voice sympathetic. "I didn't mean to hurt you. I just wanted you to understand that this world is real."

"No!" Stacy cried, fighting the panic rising inside her. "No, I must get back!" She placed her hands on the mirror's flat surface. It reflected only her face and the room behind her, and it was as solid as a wall. "Please," she begged Philomena. "Please tell me how the mirror works. I have to go back to my own home!"

For a moment Philomena looked angry, but then she appeared puzzled. "Truly I don't know what you're talking about," she said. "How can a mirror 'work'?"

"But I came here through the mirror," Stacy insisted. "Don't you remember? You took my hands and pulled me through!"

Again Philomena looked puzzled. "Oh, no," she said. "That's not what happened. You are here because I wished for you. I've been wishing for you for a long time. Ever since my sister died I've been wishing for a dear friend to replace her." She gently took Stacy's hand. "Don't look so unhappy," she said. "You will be happy here, I promise. Now come sit down and let me make you a cup of tea."

Confused, Stacy let Philomena lead her to the kitchen table. Everything in the room was new, even though every item had been made in an earlier century. There were no gleaming modern appliances, no refrigerator or dishwasher. In fact, there were no appliances at all. A large metal tub stood on a high table where a sink might be in a modern kitchen. Fascinated, Stacy watched while Philomena placed some herbs in a cup, then poured water into it from a large teakettle that was simmering on top of the wood-burning stove.

"Drink this," Philomena said. "It will make you feel better."

Stacy took a sip of the tea, which was fragrant with spices. Almost immediately she did feel better. *I've got to stay calm,* she told herself. *I've got to relax and observe and try to figure out what's happened. That's the only way I'll be able to get back home.*

"Are you feeling better?" Philomena asked, sitting next to her.

"Yes, thank you," said Stacy. "But tell me, Philomena. Where am I? And—And what year is this?"

"You're in Phantom Valley," Philomena answered. "The first settlers began coming here a dozen years ago. My parents were among them. And the year is 1851."

Eighteen fifty-one! Stacy could hardly believe her ears. Somehow, she had gone back in time more than a hundred forty years! She glanced out the window at the pine forest. Just above the trees the moon illuminated the cliffs of Canyon Ridge, which were also just visible from Chilleen Academy. *I don't believe it*, she thought. *If this weren't so scary, it would be fascinating.*

"How long have you lived here?" she asked Philomena.

"Why, my whole life," Philomena answered. "My parents were taken by illness when I was young. I live with my grandmother. This is her farm, and we work it together."

"Are you very near Silverbell?" Stacy asked, still trying to place the farm.

"Silverbell is quite far from here," Philomena said. "It is a good day's journey by wagon. We go there twice a year to get supplies."

Stacy thought for a moment about what Philomena had said. What a strange, isolated life she led! "What about school?" she asked. "Where do you go to school?"

Philomena laughed, a musical sound. "Why would I go to school?" she asked. "My grandmother has taught me to read and write. That is all I require."

"Where do your friends live?"

Philomena's eyes filled with tears. "Alas, I have none," she said. "The only farms in walking distance are worked by old people with no children. My dear sister was my friend, the best friend a girl could have. But since she died there has been no one for me."

"That's very sad," Stacy said.

"But now that you are here, I won't be lonely any

longer," Philomena said. "I'll have you as a companion and friend—you'll be almost like a sister."

Stacy started to speak, to tell Philomena that she couldn't stay, that she must return to her own time as soon as she could figure out how. Then she remembered how Philomena had reacted when she'd mentioned the mirror, and decided to keep quiet.

"We're eating our evening meal very late tonight," Philomena said then. "Will you help me fetch some water?"

"Sure," Stacy answered.

"It's out here in the yard," said Philomena, handing Stacy a bucket. "We're lucky. Some folks have to walk several miles for water." She took the kerosene lantern and led Stacy out into the yard, then showed her how to hold the bucket steady while she began to pump from a well.

The girls carried two buckets of water into the house. Philomena poured one into a big pot and set it on top of the stove. "Grandmother is out in the barn helping to birth some piglets," she said. "I hope she will be in soon."

I hope so too, Stacy thought. *Maybe she'll be able to tell me how the mirror works so I can get out of here.*

Philomena poured a bowl of shelled peas into the water, then showed Stacy the cabinet where dishes were kept. Stacy was just starting to set the table for three when the kitchen door banged open. She turned to see the old woman standing exhausted in the doorway.

"The little ones will be fine," Philomena's grandmother said. She opened her mouth to speak again, then stopped, her eyes wide with terror. She took a step backward and stumbled.

Stacy started to go to her, to help her, but the old woman's eyes opened even wider and she began shouting, "Demon child! What are you doing here, you strange, unearthly demon child?"

CHAPTER 6

TRACY

THE next morning, Tracy woke with the feeling that she'd been having a nightmare, but she couldn't remember what it was about. Then she remembered that she was *living* a nightmare since her sister had disappeared.

Hoping against hope, she looked across the room at Stacy's bed, but it was smooth and hadn't been slept in. "No," she moaned aloud. She got out of bed and approached the mirror. Its flat, silvery surface reflected only her own unhappy face.

As she had the night before, she pulled the mirror out from the wall and checked behind it. But there was nothing there. Stacy was still gone, and Tracy knew she would have to keep her sister's disappearance a secret.

The flu epidemic at school could help her. Tracy checked her schedule and her sister's, then stepped out into the hall, where there was a telephone.

Looking around guiltily, Tracy punched in the extension for the infirmary. After a moment Mrs. Albert, the school nurse, answered.

"This is Stacy James," she said into the phone. "I woke up with a bad sore throat and headache. I don't think I can go to my classes this morning."

"The flu is going around," the nurse told her. "In fact, all the beds in the infirmary are being used. Come on down and let me take a look at you."

Tracy quickly pulled on a pair of jeans and one of Stacy's green T-shirts before combing her hair straight like Stacy's. She studied herself critically in the mirror, then applied a light dusting of blush all over her face to make herself look feverish. Thinking sick, she made her way down to the first floor infirmary.

The main room of the infirmary was crowded with beds filled with students. All the kids were talking at once, calling for the nurse and across the room to one another. Tracy went into the examining room. Mrs. Albert frowned distractedly when she saw her. "Oh, dear," she said. "You do look a little flushed." She placed her hand on Stacy's forehead. "Doesn't seem to be much of a fever," she went on. She stared down into Tracy's throat, making *mm-hmm* sounds. Then she pressed her fingers into Tracy's neck just under her ears. "Sit still for a few moments," she said, popping a thermometer into Tracy's mouth. "I've got to check on my other patients," she said. "I'll be right back."

As soon as Mrs. Albert went into the next room, Tracy stepped over to the sink and ran hot water on the thermometer. When it reached 101 degrees, she stuck it back into her mouth and returned to her seat. She could hear the voices of other kids in the main room.

"Let's see now," Mrs. Albert said when she returned. She examined the thermometer for a moment, her eyebrows arching in surprise. "Why you do have a bit of a fever," she said. "Sometimes a cool cheek can fool you." She stood back and regarded Tracy with a worried expression. "I don't know what to do with you," she said. "I don't have a bed for you in the infirmary right now."

"That's okay," said Tracy, thinking how lucky she was. "I don't mind staying in my room."

"Are you sure?" Mrs. Albert asked. Tracy nodded. "Well, it's settled then. I'll come check on you this afternoon, and I'll make arrangements for someone to bring you your meals on a tray."

"That's okay," Tracy said. "My sister can do it."

"Very well," said Mrs. Albert, handing her two Tylenol tablets. "Take these and try to get some rest. I'll see you around four."

Tracy hurried back to her room, thanking her good fortune. Now she wouldn't have to worry about being Stacy until later in the afternoon, when Mrs. Albert came to check on her.

She was just about to change into her own clothes when there was a knock at the door.

"Who is it?" she called, her heart pounding.

"It's us," came an uncomfortingly familiar voice. "Angela and Dorie. We've come to pick Stacy up for breakfast."

Tracy froze. She hadn't known that Stacy was supposed to go to breakfast with Angela. "Just a minute!" she called. She took a deep breath to calm herself and then opened the door a crack and stuck her head out. "Hi," she said, trying to sound normal. "Stacy's down in the infirmary. She's sick."

Angela gave her a strange look.

"Well, do you want to come eat with us?" Dorie asked.

Tracy declined, and the two girls left. Tracy quickly changed into her own clothes and fixed her hair. She barely had time to get to the dining room for a quick breakfast before running off to her first class.

When she walked into the classroom, she imagined that everyone was staring at her. *This is ridiculous*, she told herself. *I don't have anything to worry about.* But she couldn't shake the uneasy feeling that other people would be able to tell something was wrong.

For the rest of the morning Tracy tried to concentrate on what the teachers were saying, but it was hard. Her mind kept drifting back to her room, and the mirror, and the terror in Stacy's eyes when the young girl had pulled her into the mirror.

After each of her classes Tracy stopped by Stacy's classes to pick up her assignments for the next day. The teachers were really piling it on. Midterms were to be the next week. Tracy knew she'd have to keep Stacy's work up as well as her own. Her sister was such a good student that her teachers would suspect something was wrong if Stacy's grades fell.

"Hey, Tracy!" Tracy jumped as a hand tapped her shoulder. She whirled around to see Cissy Davis, a friend of hers and Stacy's.

"Oh, hi, Cissy," Tracy said, relieved. "What's up?"

"Not much," said Cissy. "I heard from Angela that Stacy's sick. I thought I'd stop by and say hi to her."

"She has a sore throat," Tracy said. "The nurse thinks it might be contagious. I'll tell her you said hi."

With a friendly wave, Cissy went on to her next class.

What will I do if someone comes by to see "Stacy" when I'm not in the room? Tracy wondered.

By lunchtime she was exhausted. She took a wrapped sandwich and an apple from the lunchroom and went back to her room. The first thing she saw when she entered was the mirror. Without much hope, she approached it and gazed into its flat silvery surface. *Where are you, Stacy?* she wondered.

Just in case anyone came by, she took her hair out of its ponytail. Then she sat on Stacy's bed, eating her lunch and starting on Stacy's math homework for the next day. Stacy's class was a few days ahead of her own, and the problems were hard. *I'm not going to have time to do anything but homework today*, she thought.

After lunch she went back to her classes. In math, Mr. Harper gave a review quiz. Tracy hadn't really

42

studied for it. She was surprised that it was relatively easy, though. Maybe it was because she had just done harder work in Stacy's homework assignment. In fact, she finished earlier than most of the other kids, and Mr. Harper gave her a funny sideways glance when she handed her paper in.

She had volleyball practice that day after school. But first she had to make an appearance as "Stacy." She rushed back to her room, combed her hair out, and climbed into the bed just as Mrs. Albert knocked on the door.

"Good afternoon, dear," the nurse said. "How are you feeling?"

"My throat's still sore," Tracy croaked, wondering how long she was going to have to keep playing this game.

"Say aah," Mrs. Albert said, peering into her mouth. "It looks much better. I wouldn't be surprised if you're fine tomorrow."

"Maybe," said Tracy doubtfully. "I've got an awful headache, though."

"Well, we'll see," said the nurse. "In the meantime, don't get too close to anyone."

"I won't, I promise," Tracy said.

For a few moments after Mrs. Albert left, she just lay in bed. She didn't have time to just lie around, though. She had to get busy. Changing into shorts, she went out to the volleyball court.

Several girls and boys greeted her as she took her place in the back row. Angela, who was on the other side, gave her a big smile. "How's Stacy?" she called across the court. "Stacy's sick with flu," Angela explained to the other kids.

"She's just fine," said Tracy, wishing Angela would stop being such a busybody.

"Tell her I'll come visit her this evening," Angela said. "Maybe a bunch of us ought to come."

"I don't think she feels like having visitors," Tracy said quickly.

She tossed the ball and just for a moment imagined it was Angela's head. Hitting as hard as she could, she served the ball straight into the center of the opposite court for an ace.

By nine-thirty that night Tracy felt as if she had lived through three weeks in one day. She couldn't remember ever having had such a busy day. As soon as she'd eaten her supper, she went back up to her room and began working on homework—first Stacy's, then her own. With a pang she thought of the other kids watching TV in the dayroom.

Stacy's reading assignment for history was long and boring. But Tracy forced herself to concentrate on it from start to finish, and even to answer all the questions at the end. *How does Stacy manage to do this?* she wondered.

As she worked, she kept glancing at the mirror, hoping that the other room would return and that Stacy would be in it. At last, just as she was finishing her own history reading, she saw a flicker of movement in the mirror. She immediately shut her book. This was her chance.

She had a plan for rescuing Stacy. Remembering the way the girl in the mirror had reached out to her sister, Tracy planned to do the same if she saw Stacy. But would it work? Would Stacy even be there?

CHAPTER 7

STACY

"**D**EMON-CHILD!" cried the old woman again. Suddenly she snatched up a carving knife from the table.

Her heart pounding, Stacy took a step back. The old woman followed, shaking the knife at her.

"Gran—" Philomena started to say, but the woman stopped her.

"Where did you come from?" she demanded. "What mischief do you mean here?"

"I didn't mean to come here at all," Stacy tried to explain. "I don't intend to do anything but—"

"She comes from a far distant land," Philomena said quickly. "She was sleeping in her parents' wagon and accidentally fell out while they were passing through Phantom Valley."

"Is this true?" asked the grandmother.

"Yes," Stacy said, not knowing what else to say.

"Then why are you dressed in those clothes?"

Stacy looked down at herself and immediately knew why the grandmother was so upset. She seemed to have come from nowhere, and her jeans and T-shirt must have looked to the old woman the way a Martian's clothes would look to Stacy.

"It's the costume of her native land," Philomena explained. "I'll let her wear my other dress, and she'll look just like us."

The old woman slowly put down the carving knife. "I'm sorry, child," she said. "But we can't be too careful out here all alone. And of course there was all that trouble with the others."

"Grandmother means some other people who visited us once," Philomena said nervously. "They were a lot of bother." She turned quickly to the old woman. "I promise there won't be any trouble," Philomena assured her.

"Nevertheless," said the grandmother, "it'll be better for all of us if this child's parents return for her as soon as possible."

The next morning the old woman, Granny Johnson, woke the girls as soon as the sun was up. "Come on, girls," she said. "It's time to begin the chores." She opened the curtains, then turned to Stacy, a weary smile on her face. "I hope you don't mind helping out, young lady. We work hard here."

"Of course I don't mind," Stacy answered, figuring that she had no choice.

"Good," said the old woman. "For this morning, then, you can draw the water for the weekly wash. After that, you can scrub the floors and do the mending. By then it should be time to feed the chickens and slop the hogs. Can you do all that?"

"Yes," Stacy answered, though she wasn't really sure she could.

"Don't worry," Philomena said. "I'll help you."

The old woman left then, her old shoulders rounded and stooped.

"Your grandmother's nice, but kind of gruff," Stacy told Philomena.

"Yes. Don't believe much of what she says," Philomena said. "She has dreams and she mixes them up with life."

"Oh," said Stacy, disappointed. She was hoping for an opportunity to ask the grandmother about the mirror.

"Come on, Stacy," Philomena said cheerfully. "We'd best get started on the chores."

For the next several hours Stacy was far too busy with chores to think of the mirror or anything else.

The first chore, drawing water, she had done before, but she was shocked at the number of buckets needed for the weekly wash. She and Philomena pumped bucket after bucket, carrying them to a huge wooden washtub on the back porch. As she worked, Stacy thought about how difficult life had been for the pioneers, and how different from the life she was used to. The next chore, scrubbing the floor, was something she had done for her mother many times. But instead of a sponge mop, she and Philomena used rags and a heavy scrub brush. Instead of a detergent that washed and waxed at the same time, they had to dip rags into a pail of water containing a bar of strong, nasty-smelling lye soap that burned their hands and made them turn red.

The house wasn't big, but it took a long time to scrub. By the time the girls had finished with the floor, it was late morning. "We'd all best eat something," the grandmother announced, coming in from the porch, where she'd been doing the laundry. Stacy realized that she was starving, and thought a juicy cheeseburger or a slice of pizza would hit the spot. But instead Granny Johnson handed her a plate containing a cold biscuit and a greasy slab of something rubbery looking.

"What is that?" she asked.

"Salt pork," Philomena said. "It's delicious."

Hesitantly, Stacy tried the cold slab of meat. It tasted worse than it looked, and was so tough and salty she couldn't swallow it. "Do you have anything else?" she asked after two bites.

The grandmother's distress was evident. "I'm sorry," she said. "Salt pork is what we have, and salt pork is what we eat."

"It's okay, I wasn't very hungry anyway," said Stacy. But her stomach was growling. *I don't belong in this world*, she thought. *Somehow, I've got to find a way to get back home.*

After lunch Granny went back to the laundry while Philomena got the basket of mending. It was the first time Stacy had been alone in the main room. Her eyes fell on the mirror, pushed up against the wall opposite the hearth.

As she noted the night before, it was identical to the mirror that stood in her room at school. The only difference was that the glass and wood were new on this mirror. *It must be the same mirror*, she thought.

She approached it and peered in, longing to see her room at the Chilleen Academy. But all that was reflected back was her own face, streaked with sweat and dirt, and her blue eyes, rimmed with tears. She reached out and touched the mirror's flat, hard surface. Somewhere beyond the mirror, she knew, was home and her sister. *Maybe tonight*, she thought, *I'll be able to go back*.

The rest of the afternoon the girls sewed patches on clothing, sheets, and towels. Many of the things were badly worn, she noticed. She would just have thrown them away. Here, she knew, nothing could ever be wasted. *What a hard way to live*, she thought.

As they worked, Philomena told Stacy about her life in Phantom Valley and about how she and her sister had worked together happily. They hadn't played much, Philomena explained, because there was so much work to do. Stacy could sense how lonely Philomena was.

"I have a sister too," she confided to Philomena. "I miss her very much."

"Then you know how happy I am to have you here," said Philomena with a big smile.

By the end of the day, when Stacy was so exhausted

from doing chores that she felt as if she might fall asleep on her feet, it was time to feed the chickens and hogs. Once again she and Philomena pumped water from the well, then carried it to the hogs. Next they carried huge sacks of feed for the chickens, and heavy buckets of slop for the hogs.

As she sat in the dimly lit room that evening, Stacy could only pick at her meal of boiled potatoes, cold biscuits, and salt pork. She was too tired to eat. *I must stay awake till later,* she kept telling herself. *I must see if Tracy will appear in the mirror. Maybe then I can go back.*

Philomena and her grandmother went to bed early. Stacy lay beside Philomena on her narrow, lumpy bed, willing herself to stay awake. Once she was certain that Philomena was deeply asleep, she crept out of bed and into the main room.

Her heart pounding with excitement, Stacy tiptoed toward the mirror. The moon had not yet risen, and it was very dark, but Stacy could clearly see the outline of the mirror. *Please,* she thought, *please let it show me pictures of home. Please let it be working. Please.* But instead of Tracy and her dorm room, all she saw was the darkened kitchen.

As she had earlier in the day, Stacy felt the mirror's surface, hoping to find a way to pass through it. It was just an ordinary and very solid piece of glass now.

Disappointment lumped in her throat. "No," she whispered. "No, I want to go home."

"What is it, dear Stacy?" Philomena was right behind her.

"Philomena!" Stacy said, whirling around in surprise. "I didn't hear you."

"When I saw you had left the bed, I had to come find you," Philomena said. "Is anything wrong?"

"Everything's wrong!" Stacy said, beginning to cry. "I miss school, and my sister. I want to go back! Oh, Philomena, please help me get home where I belong."

Philomena came closer and took Stacy's hand in her own. "But dear friend Stacy," she said, "you do belong here. Don't you understand? You're my friend now, and you'll never ever leave here."

CHAPTER 8

TRACY

IT was almost a week since Stacy had disappeared, and Tracy still couldn't believe it. She kept expecting to wake up to find Stacy in her bed and everything the way it should be. Except nothing was the way it was supposed to be.

Tracy was exhausted. Whenever she and Stacy had pretended to be each other in the past, it had been fun and done only as a joke. Never before had she had to do it seriously, and she would never have believed how hard it could be.

Most of the past week, Tracy had been able to use the flu to her advantage. For the first three days "Stacy" had been sick, and for the next two, "Tracy" had been sick. She had gone to classes as whichever twin was supposed to be well and posed as the "sick" twin in the early morning and late afternoon when the nurse visited.

In the evenings she had been too busy studying to socialize. So whenever anyone dropped by, she simply pretended to be sick. So far no one had figured out what she was doing. But Angela was making her nervous. She was Stacy's best friend, and she was acting especially nosy. *I'll have to be very careful around Angela,* she realized.

Monday would begin the two-week midterm exam period. Regular classes were canceled, with optional study sessions instead. Tracy realized she could go to a study session for either twin and not have to explain any absences, which should make her life a lot easier. Luckily, neither twin had exams during the same hour, but the thought of taking two sets of exams made Tracy almost sick. *I've got to get her back as soon as possible,* she thought. *I've got to!*

The next morning, Monday, Tracy had to force herself to get out of bed. It had been a rainy night, and she'd stayed up late, waiting for the room in the mirror to appear. It never did. Yawning, she checked Stacy's and her schedules to decide which study sessions she needed to attend. She was relieved that she would not have to pretend to be sick anymore. Her only real problem would be appearing twice for meals, once as each twin.

She decided to attend the first sessions as herself, then switch and be Stacy in the afternoon. That way everyone would see "both" twins and wouldn't become suspicious.

After her last class of the morning, she rushed to the dining room, signed in, and ate a very light meal as herself. Then she excused herself, went back to her room, changed her clothes and hairdo, and came down for a sandwich as "Stacy."

She chose a ham-and-cheese sandwich and was about to sit down at an empty table to eat it when she heard Stacy's name being called.

"We're over here!" Angela yelled from across the room. "Where are you going?"

"I was so late, I thought you'd be finished," Tracy said, bringing her tray to Angela's table.

"You're always busy lately," Angela said. "And you missed a great pizza party in Dorie's room last night. Why didn't you come?"

"I—I had to study," said Tracy.

"Really?" Angela said. "I can understand your sister having to, but not you."

"Well, that's how I keep my grades up," Tracy said.

For a moment Angela didn't answer. With a guilty start, Tracy thought she looked suspicious again. "By the way," Angela went on, "do you have any ideas for Sunday night?"

"What do you mean?" Tracy asked.

"You know," said Angela. "At least you ought to know—it was your idea in the first place!"

"Oh, *that*," Tracy said, pretending to know what Angela was talking about. "Well, why don't we discuss it later?"

"All right," Angela said. "I'll come up to your room before lights out—and you'd better not forget!"

That night Tracy had a harder time than ever concentrating on her studies. She kept peeking at the mirror. At last the old kitchen began to appear.

Something was wrong, though. The kitchen was completely empty and very dim. There was no sign of Stacy, no sign of anyone. Where was her sister?

Suddenly there was a knock on the door.

"Who is it?" Tracy cried, startled.

"It's me, Angela!" came a voice. "Stacy?"

"Just a minute!" Tracy called. She had completely forgotten that Angela was coming by to talk to Stacy. She took another glance at the mirror, then ran to the door. Somehow, she had to make Angela go away without coming into the room.

She took a deep breath, then opened the door with a big smile on her face. "Hi," she said, staying in the doorway.

Angela smiled back, but she acted puzzled. "Stace?" she said.

"Yes," said Tracy, puzzled herself.

"Why are you wearing a ponytail?"

Tracy had forgotten to change her hair. "I didn't mean to confuse you," she said smoothly, "but I got hot studying and wanted to get my hair off my neck. Tracy and I don't *always* wear our hair different."

"I guess not," said Angela. "Anyway, are you ready to talk about the History Honor Society party?"

So that's what this was all about, Tracy thought. "I'm sorry," she said. "I've got too much studying to do. And, uh, I promised to help Tracy study too."

"Where is she?" asked Angela, peeking past Tracy into the room.

"She went to get her laundry," Tracy said, blocking Angela's view. "She'll be back any second."

"This won't take long," Angela said. "I'll leave when she gets back." Before Tracy could do anything to stop her, Angela had pushed her way into the room.

Please, Tracy thought. *Please don't let her look in the mirror.*

But Angela went straight to the mirror and stopped. She stared at it a moment, then turned to Tracy. "What in the world is wrong with your mirror?" she asked.

CHAPTER 9

STACY

ALTHOUGH she'd been there only about a week, Stacy felt as if she'd lived in the world of the past for years. And she hated it. All she could think from the time she got up till she went to bed was, *I want to go home!*

But how could she? Philomena refused to discuss the mirror, and her grandmother didn't seem to know anything about its powers. "It was a wedding gift from Philomena's father to her mother," she said when Stacy questioned her about it. "I only keep it because my granddaughter likes it." Twice more since the night Philomena had caught her, Stacy had sneaked into the kitchen area hoping to see her dorm room in the mirror, but it had reflected only the room she was standing in.

Philomena was loving and cheerful, grateful for Stacy's friendship. She never complained, no matter how hard the girls had to work. But whenever Stacy mentioned going home, Philomena became a person.

One afternoon, when the girls were doing chores in the barn, Stacy mentioned that there was a barn at her school, where students tended the animals.

"Don't speak of that place to me!" Philomena suddenly shouted. "I've told you before that you will stay here with me!"

"I only meant—" Stacy started to say, but Philomena picked up a pail of slops and threw it right at Stacy, covering her with the slimy liquid.

The horrible stuff dripped onto Stacy's face. She wiped the sticky mess from around her eyes and mouth, but could feel it start to thicken in her hair.

"Don't speak of it!" Philomena repeated, and stomped out of the barn.

Stacy was so furious, she was shaking. What was wrong with Philomena? All she had done was mention school. Philomena was extremely unbalanced, that was for sure. *I've got to get away from here,* Stacy thought again.

When she returned to the house a little while later, she found Philomena waiting for her outside the door. "I'm sorry, Stacy," Philomena said. "I don't know what made me act so mean. It's just that you're so dear to me. Will you forgive me?"

Stacy nodded. "I guess so," she said. She realized that she would have to be more careful than ever about what she did and said until she had a chance to escape.

"Hurry it up, girls!" Granny Johnson called through the open door. "It's time to prepare the evening meal!"

As Philomena took her hand in a friendly way, Stacy sighed and followed the other girl inside. *From now on,* she thought, *I'll just pretend that I'm happy to stay here. But somehow, and soon, I've got to find a way to get home!*

She had very little time to examine the mirror. When she wasn't busy with chores, Stacy sometimes sneaked longing glances at it. But Philomena was watchful, and Stacy was afraid of making her angry again.

Her chance to examine the mirror came one afternoon when Granny Johnson asked her to polish all the furniture. She handed Stacy a pail of foul-smelling oil and told her to wipe every inch of the woodwork.

Luckily, Philomena was helping her grandmother with the laundry outside. As soon as they left the kitchen, Stacy went to the mirror and, dipping the rag in the oil, pretended to polish it. As she did, she pressed her fingers over every part of the frame, searching for hidden buttons to make it work.

When she got to the top of the mirror, she paid special attention to the carvings of the phases of the moon. She pressed each of them and tried to move them, but nothing happened. Perhaps there was something *behind* the mirror . . . She pulled it out from the wall and was just examining the back when the kitchen door banged open.

"What are you doing!" Philomena was enraged.

"Just—just polishing the mirror, as your grandmother asked me to do," Stacy said.

"Oh, yes, of course," said Philomena, her voice calm again. "Here, let me help you." She took the rag from Stacy and began to wipe the back.

"It's a beautiful mirror," Stacy said easily, hoping to get some information about it from Philomena. "Where did it come from?"

Philomena gave her a suspicious glance, then shrugged. "It has been in our family," she said. "I believe that my great-uncle carved it."

"Was he an astronomer?" Stacy asked.

"A what?" said Philomena.

"A person who studies the stars and planets," Stacy asked. "I only wondered because of the carvings of the moon."

"Those mean nothing," Philomena said quickly. "They're just decorations."

"It's just that they are so unusual," Stacy went on, sure from Philomena's response that the carvings must have something to do with the mirror's powers.

"They're nothing!" Philomena repeated, her voice rising in anger. "Do you hear me? Forget about them!"

Sighing, Stacy went on with her chores. When she had finished polishing all the furniture in the big room, it was time to start preparing dinner.

All evening she waited for a chance to get nearer to the carvings, but Philomena was keeping an unusually close eye on her. "You look so tired," Philomena said at last. "Why don't we go to bed?"

"That's a good idea," Stacy answered, yawning. Actually, she didn't feel tired at all. Maybe that night, when Philomena and her grandmother were asleep, she could slip out of Philomena's room and figure out how to use the mirror to return home.

"Yes," agreed Granny Johnson. "You had best be getting to bed. You need your rest, for there's plenty of work to be done tomorrow."

Stacy followed Philomena into her tiny bedroom in the back of the house and changed into a long white nightgown. Philomena was soon breathing deeply beside her, sound asleep. She heard the grandmother moving around in the main room, getting ready to go to bed herself. *Just a few more minutes*, Stacy thought. *And then I can go to the mirror and find my way home.*

Just a few more minutes.

THUMP! THUMP! THUMP!

Stacy sat up in bed, her heart pounding. The noise had been so loud, Philomena stirred and sleepily opened her eyes. "Someone's at the door," she murmured.

"But it's so late—" Stacy started to say.

At that moment the door to the girls' bedroom slammed open. Standing in the doorway was a very grim Granny Johnson.

"Put on your clothes, young Stacy," she said. "The marshal has come to take you away!"

CHAPTER 10

TRACY

WHAT is that?" Angela asked again, pointing at the mirror. "What's wrong?"

Tracy looked. The room inside the mirror was still deserted and dark, and the image was so dim that it would be impossible for Angela to make out anything clearly. The only reason she knew that the kitchen was there was that she'd seen it before.

"There's nothing wrong," Tracy said calmly. She pulled out a chair for Angela, facing away from the mirror. "The mirror's just old," she went on. "The woman who sold it to my aunt said it's dark because some of the silver is gone."

"It almost looks like another room's reflected in there," said Angela. Then she shrugged and sat in the chair. "You really ought to get it fixed," she said.

"We probably will," Tracy answered. She sat in a chair facing Angela and tried hard not to look at the

63

mirror. "Now, what do we need to decide about the party?"

"Well, we've agreed it's on Sunday, right?" said Angela.

"Right," said Tracy. *This is easy*, she thought. *I'll just let her tell me everything I need to know.*

"I've got the list of History Honor Society members," Angela said. "And Mr. Taylor came up with a really neat idea for a game we can play."

"Uh-huh," Tracy said, scarcely listening.

"Here's the list," Angela said, handing her a sheet of paper.

"Of what?" Tracy asked.

"Of the members. Remember you said you'd invite everyone?"

"Oh," said Tracy. "Right. Okay, I'll do it."

Angela peered closely at her. "Are you sure you're all right?" she asked. "You've been acting really out of it lately."

"I'm sorry, Angela," said Tracy. "I guess I still feel a little run-down from being sick. I'm not paying attention to everything that I should."

"That's all right," Angela said sympathetically. "But I'm getting worried about you. You haven't been acting like yourself for days. And neither has your sister."

"It's just the pressure of exams," Tracy said. "Which reminds me, I've got to get back to my studies." She stood up, and a moment later, obviously not wanting to, Angela stood too.

As she did, something moved in the mirror and Tracy

froze. The old woman had appeared, holding a lighted candle. The room was still very dim, but anyone would now be able to see that there was the image of a person in it—a person who shouldn't be there.

"I promise I'll invite everyone tomorrow," Tracy said quickly, trying to sound casual. "Thanks for coming by."

Angela didn't move, though. Behind her, the old woman crossed the room in the mirror. "Where did you say Tracy is?" Angela asked suddenly.

"Tracy?" said Tracy, more rattled than ever. "She's—she's studying with someone. Monica, I think."

"I thought you said she was doing laundry," Angela said. "Besides, Monica's down in the dayroom watching a movie. I just saw her."

"Well, I don't know where she is," Tracy said. "We don't keep track of each other every minute, you know."

"I know," said Angela. "But it just occurred to me that I haven't seen the two of you together for a long time now." She continued to stare at Tracy, suspiciously now. "Have you two had a fight?"

"No, no, nothing like that," Tracy said, trying to keep her eyes away from the mirror.

"Really? Are you sure? You know I wouldn't tell anyone about it," Angela said.

"There's nothing to tell," Tracy said. "Everything's fine."

"Well, if you ever want to talk about it, you know

you can come to me," said Angela. "I'm going to try to come by more often, to see if I can help you."

Tracy gave up trying to convince Angela that she and her sister hadn't had a fight. Instead she just opened the door and said, "Thanks for coming."

With a last suspicious look, Angela left. Tracy breathed a sigh of relief as she shut the door. *Wonderful,* she thought. *Now the biggest snoop in Phantom Valley is going to be following me around like a puppy dog.*

She couldn't worry about it then, though. She rushed back to the mirror. At first it just showed a darkened room. Then the old woman appeared again, and a moment later Stacy joined her.

It was hard to see what was happening because the images were dim, but she could make out Stacy's hand as it suddenly shot up to her mouth. Seemingly terrified, she then backed up. At the same moment something large and dark began to approach her. Straining to see, Tracy finally realized what the dark thing was. It was the faint but unmistakable image of a big and burly man. In his outstretched hand was a long pistol, and it was pointed straight at Stacy.

CHAPTER 11

STACY

STACY walked into the kitchen area, shaking, while Marshal Briggs, a tall, severe-looking man, held a pistol on her. Granny Johnson had lit a kerosene lamp so the marshal could take a good look at Stacy. He immediately lowered his gun.

"Beg pardon, miss," he said. "You're not the one I'm looking for."

"I believe she's a runaway," said the old woman.

"You've had runaways stay here before, as I recall," the marshal said.

"She's my friend!" cried Philomena. "Don't take her!"

"I don't have any intention of taking her," Marshal Briggs said. "I'm searching for Miss Annabelle Durac, who ran off the other day. I'd heard of a strange girl staying out here on your farm, but this one's at least five years too young."

"Annabelle Durac!" sniffed Granny Johnson. "Why didn't you say so? If you ask me, she probably ran off with that cowboy beau of hers."

"Most likely," agreed the marshal. "But I promised her parents I'd look for her. Now, if you'll excuse me, I'll get on back to town."

Stacy stared after him as he went out the door, her mind swirling with a thousand thoughts. Who were the runaways the marshal had mentioned? What had happened to them? Had other girls come through the mirror before her? She glanced over at Philomena, who was smiling happily.

"Oh, Stacy," she said. "I was so frightened. I was so afraid you'd leave me too."

Too? Stacy thought. How many people had left her? She wondered. And where had they gone?

That night Stacy dreamed of the mirror. In her dream she could see into it, see the cozy little room she had shared with Tracy at Chilleen. But when she tried to reach through it, to clasp Tracy's hand, the silvery surface of the mirror began to dissolve, like ice in the spring. With it, her room at Chilleen and Tracy dissolved too.

She awoke before sunrise, more determined than ever to discover the secret of the mirror. Stacy knew that Philomena would never tell her, so she'd have to find the truth herself. She slipped out of bed and, tiptoeing into the cold kitchen area, headed straight for the mirror.

At a sudden sound she turned to see Philomena standing at the bedroom door. Philomena's eyes were dark with anger, but in an instant her face relaxed into its usual loving smile. "Why are you up so early, Stacy?" she asked. "Were you thinking to get an early start making breakfast? Here, I'll help you."

That afternoon, Stacy and Philomena did the ironing for the week. Of course there was no electric iron. Granny Johnson had a pair of heavy, cast-iron flatirons that were heated on the wood-burning stove. Stacy and Philomena took turns ironing the sheets and clothing with one while the other was heating.

Once I get back to my own time, I'll never complain about housework again, Stacy thought. Despite all her reading in history, she had never imagined that life was so difficult for settlers in the Old West.

She finished folding some freshly ironed clothes as Philomena ironed another batch. "Where do these go?" she asked Philomena, gathering up the bundle.

"Put them in the wardrobe," Philomena said. She had been tired and cranky all day, probably because she'd been awakened the night before.

Stacy took the bundle of clothes into Philomena's room and pulled open the heavy wooden door to the large wardrobe. She began to push Philomena's things aside to make room for the freshly ironed clothes, then realized that she had never checked out the inside of the wardrobe. Maybe there was a key or a set of instructions to the mirror.

After glancing back over her shoulder, Stacy moved more things aside. She ran her hand along the shelves at the top. At first she didn't feel anything and was about to close the door, but then her hand closed around a long package wrapped in layer after layer of old towels. It was heavy, and she pulled it slowly from the wardrobe and began to unwind the layers of cloth. She had it nearly unwrapped before she realized what it was and almost dropped it in surprise.

The object in her hands was an axe. Her hands shaking, Stacy examined it more closely and saw that the blade was covered with faint brown stains that could be dried blood.

If it was blood, whose was it? And what was the axe doing in Philomena's closet? For a moment Stacy felt panic closing off her throat and she could hardly breathe. *I've got to get out of here,* she thought again. *I can't wait any longer!*

CHAPTER 12

TRACY

ALL the next day and evening Tracy was frantic with worry about Stacy. She had watched, helpless and horrified, the night before, while the tall man held a gun on her sister. After a moment he did lower the pistol at least. Before Tracy had been able to find out what had happened, though, the image disappeared and the mirror went blank.

What had happened to her sister? she wondered. Who had the man been? Could he have taken Stacy away with him?

She hardly slept that night, and found it more difficult than usual during the day to pretend to be her sister or to remember who she was supposed to be. While sitting in on a Spanish review class, she had even fallen asleep.

As soon as Tracy returned to her room after dinner that evening, she rushed to the mirror, but all it reflected was her own lonely room. While waiting for the images to appear, Tracy began to study for her next test, which was Stacy's math midterm. She opened the book to the practice problems and began to work. *Funny*, she thought. *A couple of weeks ago I didn't have a clue how to do these problems, and now they seem easy.*

She was just checking the mirror again when there was a knock at the door. *If it's that snoop Angela*, she thought, *I'm going to throw something at her.* She fluffed up her ponytail and pulled on one of Stacy's green sweatshirts, before going to the door. To her surprise, a very serious Mrs. Danita stood there.

"Stacy?" she asked.

"No, I'm Tracy," said Tracy, not thinking. "I'm— I'm just wearing one of Stacy's sweatshirts."

"Well, I had hoped to talk to both of you," the headmistress said.

"Stacy's studying with one of her friends," Tracy said. "I'm not sure who."

"That's partly what I want to talk to you about," Mrs. Danita said. "The two of you seem to be having some problems lately. Is there anything you want to talk to me about?"

For just a moment Tracy considered telling Mrs. Danita about the whole thing. The headmistress was kind and might be able to help her. But she realized there was no way to explain it without both twins getting in serious trouble. *Well, you see, Mrs. Danita, it all started when Stacy took the history quiz for me. . . .* If she didn't get in trouble, the headmistress would probably think she was crazy. *Well, yes, I do have a problem, Mrs. Danita. You see, my sister has disappeared into a mirror. . . .*

"Tracy?" Mrs. Danita repeated. "Is there something wrong?"

"No, nothing," said Tracy finally, trying to look innocent and normal. "Doesn't everyone have a hard time during exams?"

"Mrs. Pacheco told me that you fell asleep during the Spanish review class today," Mrs. Danita said. "And several teachers have noticed that both of you have been skipping some review sessions."

"We only go to the ones we really need," Tracy said. "Besides, aren't they supposed to be optional?"

"Well, yes, they are," said Mrs. Danita. "But as you know, most students take advantage of the opportunity to study for exams with the teacher."

"Well, we'll both try to do better," Tracy said.

Mrs. Danita stood staring at her a moment. "I'd really like to talk to both of you," she said. She consulted a list in her hands. "According to the schedule, the only day that neither of you has an exam is next Monday. I'd like both of you to come into my office that day before school."

"Are we in trouble?" Tracy asked.

"Not at all," Mrs. Danita said. "But I feel something is troubling you, and I'd like to get to the bottom of it."

After Mrs. Danita left, Tracy sat and stared after her. *I've got to get Stacy back before Monday*, she thought. *If not, I'll have to tell Mrs. Danita everything!*

73

CHAPTER 13

STACY

SHE forced herself to take a deep breath. *Calm down, Stacy,* she told herself sternly. *There might be a perfectly good reason for the axe.* She carefully rewrapped it. Maybe it was the axe they slaughtered the chickens and hogs with, she told herself. But why was Philomena keeping it in her closet?

That night Granny Johnson went to bed earlier than usual, complaining of rheumatism, and Philomena got ready to follow her. "Come on, Stacy," Philomena said irritably. "We can't stay up all night."

Stacy had been sitting in the doorway of the farmhouse, staring up at the slim sliver of the old moon. "I—I want to stay up and look at the moon awhile," Stacy said.

"The moon, the moon, is that the only thing you care about?" demanded Philomena. "I say we are going to bed now! Just to make sure you stay in bed, I'm going to lock the door!"

Feeling hopeless and frightened, Stacy followed Philomena into the bedroom and slipped into her nightgown. To Stacy's horror, Philomena removed the key from the leather cord she always wore around her neck and turned it in the lock. Then she settled into bed. Within minutes she was sound asleep.

Stacy lay silently beside the other girl, trying to get up the courage to do what she must. At last she slowly began to untie the cord around the sleeping girl's neck. Philomena stirred, and Stacy dropped the cord. Philomena only turned over, however, still sound asleep. Stacy found it easier to undo the knot after Philomena shifted, and finally she slipped the key off. Then she crept out of bed and unlocked the door.

The light was quite dim, but Stacy knew exactly where the mirror stood. Not daring to risk lighting a candle or lantern, she tiptoed up to it. A thin shaft of light from the old moon fell in front of the mirror. As before, the mirror was only a mirror, reflecting the kitchen.

Stacy was certain that the secret to the mirror's power had to do with the carvings at the top of the frame. She examined them closely. The woman at the flea market had said they represented the phases of the moon. The two round circles on each end must represent the full moon and new moon, she realized. The light-colored circle would be the full moon, while the dark one would be the new moon, the time of the month when the moon was completely dark.

Stacy began to press on the different carvings, first one at a time, then in combination. She tried almost all the combinations before deciding to press the carvings of the old moon and the new moon at the same time. There was a muffled *click*, and then, to her excitement, Stacy saw a pale image begin to form inside the mirror's silvered surface.

The scene inside the mirror was very dim, but her heart leaped excitedly when she recognized the outlines of her bed and study table in her room back at Chilleen. A moment later Tracy's face suddenly appeared.

Stacy was too excited to see her sister to do anything but stare, tears forming in her eyes. Tracy looked tired, she saw, and unhappy, probably from worrying about her. And then suddenly Tracy's expression changed to one of joy. She recognized Stacy on the other side of the mirror.

They could see each other! That meant they might be able to touch each other, and Stacy could go home. She reached out for the silvery surface at the same moment that Tracy did. Her fingers only touched hard glass. Maybe Tracy had to do something with the carvings of the moon on the other side, she thought. "Look," she said, exaggerating her lip movements. She pointed above her, to the carvings on the top of the mirror. At first Tracy seemed puzzled. Then she lifted her arm and reached up to the top of the frame on her side as well.

"The moon," Stacy said, again hoping Tracy could read her lips. "The new moon and the full moon."

Again Tracy seemed puzzled. Finally she did repeat the word *moon*.

Excited, Stacy nodded yes, then repeated, "New moon," She was about to add, "Full moon," when she heard a noise behind her. Her heart pounding, she whirled around to see an angry Philomena standing in the bedroom doorway.

"Philomena, I—" she started to say.

Philomena didn't wait for her to finish. She darted toward the stove, picked up one of the flatirons, and threw it straight at the mirror.

CHAPTER 14

STACY

MOVING more quickly than she thought possible, Stacy pushed the mirror to the side. Just as she did, the heavy iron whirred past her head and crashed against the wall.

Philomena came slowly toward her, looking quite mad. "You're trying to leave me!" she cried.

"No, no," Stacy protested. "It's not that at all!"

Philomena picked up the flatiron. "Get away from the mirror," she ordered.

"Philomena, no, please," Stacy pleaded. "Let me explain—"

"I won't allow you to leave!" Philomena cried.

Stacy just stared at Philomena in horror. Then she got an idea. "But I don't want to leave!" she said.

"You don't?"

"That's what I tried to tell you!" Stacy cried. "I love it here. But I get so homesick sometimes." She began to cry. "Don't you understand?" she went on. "I can't help missing my old home. I can't help wondering how everything is there. I only want to see it."

"That's all?" asked Philomena suspiciously.

"Honestly," Stacy said, still sobbing. "I—I could be completely happy here, Philomena, I really could, if only I knew that my sister—"

"What about your sister?" asked Philomena, no longer suspicious.

"I just want to be sure that she's all right," Stacy said. "We've always been so close."

"My sister and I were close too," Philomena said, her gray eyes brimming with tears. "I never loved another person so much. She was my best friend, until she died."

"I know how you feel," Stacy said. "I feel that way about my sister too." To Stacy's relief, Philomena set the flatiron back on the hearth. Stacy then followed her to the table, where they both sat. *I've got to convince her I'm on her side*, Stacy thought. *Otherwise I'll never learn the secret of the mirror.*

"My sister's name was Melody," Philomena said.

"That's a beautiful name," Stacy said.

"She was as beautiful as her name," said Philomena. "I'll never stop missing her if I live to be a hundred years old." She studied Stacy closely, then took her hand. "But now that you're here, you're my best friend, aren't you, Stacy?"

"Yes," Stacy said. "I am."

"You can never be my sister," Philomena went

on, "but you can take her place. Do you understand?"

"Yes," said Stacy. "Yes, I do understand."

Philomena continued to hold Stacy's hand, her expression sad and wistful. Suddenly she squeezed Stacy's hand and stared hard at her. "But you won't leave like the others," she said. "I won't let you leave the way they tried."

"The others?" Stacy said, bewildered. This was the second time Philomena had talked about "others."

"Never you mind," said Philomena, her voice changing from sweet to harsh. "They all learned their lessons, every one of them."

"Will you tell me a little bit about them?" Stacy asked. "So I don't make the same mistakes they did?"

"Just don't try to leave and you'll be all right," Philomena said. "Do you understand?"

"Yes," Stacy answered. "I promise I won't ever leave you, Philomena." She paused, and took a deep breath. "Only . . ." She let the thought trail off.

"Only what?" said Philomena. "I thought you said you wanted to stay here."

"I do, I do," Stacy said. "But as I told you, I can't be completely happy until I know that my sister's all right. And how can I be your best friend if I'm not happy?"

"I'm sorry," Philomena said. "I know you miss your sister, but I cannot allow you to visit her."

"Not visit her," Stacy said quickly. "I just want to

see her. To look at her through the mirror to be sure that she's happy and well."

"That's all you want?" Philomena asked. "Just to see her?"

"That's all," Stacy said. "So can't you tell me the secret of the mirror? Just to let me take a peek into my old world?"

Philomena thought in silence a moment, then sighed out loud. "Very well," she said. "I will allow you to look through the mirror, just once, to be sure that everything is all right."

"Oh, thank you!" cried Stacy. She threw her arms around Philomena and hugged her. "When can I do it? Tonight?"

"Oh, no," Philomena said, laughing. "You'll have to wait till Sunday. The image in the mirror will be very dim tonight. You'd scarcely be able to see your sister."

"Why would it be dim?" Stacy asked.

"Look out the window," Philomena said. "Do you see how thin the moon is tonight? Well, the brighter the moon, the brighter the image, and the reverse is also true. Also, the pictures can only be seen when the moon itself shines upon the mirror."

"Then—Sunday the images should be even dimmer," Stacy said, trying to hide her disappointment. "It will be the new moon then and there will be no moonlight at all."

"That is correct," Philomena said, "but there is a special power about the new moon. During that time the image is as bright as during the full moon. The pictures in the mirror can be seen despite the lack of moonlight."

"When I came here, it was during the full moon!" Stacy remembered with sudden excitement.

"Yes," Philomena said. "You are very clever to understand that."

"Is that the secret of traveling through the mirror?" Stacy asked. "That it can only be done when the image is brightest?"

"Yes," Philomena said. "I don't know why it is so, but that is the way it is. It can only be done at the new moon or the full moon. In fact, often—" She stopped talking abruptly, suspicious once again. "But I thought you only wanted to look," she said, a hard edge to her voice.

"That *is* all I want," Stacy said hastily. "I promise. I was just curious about the workings of the mirror."

"Well, I suppose there is no harm in letting you look during the new moon Sunday night," Philomena said.

"Thank you," Stacy said.

"You will be able to see very clearly then. But take a good, long look, one that will last you forever." Philomena paused, then smiled. "After you have seen your sister—I will smash the mirror to bits."

Stacy listened to Philomena with horror. She didn't doubt that the girl would do what she said. She knew that Sunday night—at the new moon—would be her only chance to escape.

CHAPTER 15.

TRACY

TRACY allowed herself to sleep late on Sunday morning because neither she nor Stacy had a test until Tuesday. When she got back from breakfast, she started to study for Stacy's English grammar test, but couldn't keep her mind on it. Instead, she kept thinking about seeing Stacy in the mirror a few nights before.

She was trying to tell me something, Tracy thought for the hundredth time. *She was trying to tell me the secret of the mirror.*

She yawned, got up from her desk, and moved in front of the mirror. She carefully examined the carvings on the frame once again. The phases of the moon ranged from tiny slivers to the round images of the full and new moons. What had Stacy been trying to tell her? she wondered.

She remembered that when Stacy had pointed to the frame, her hands had been near the carved images of the new and full moons. Those images were also much bigger than the others. *That had to be the key*, Tracy decided. *The secret of the mirror had to do with either the full moon or the new moon.*

Somewhere she'd seen pictures of the moon in all its phases. Then it came to her that she'd seen them in a book in the library.

Pulling on her shoes, she hurried across to another wing and up the stairs to the library. It was open on Sunday because of midterms. No one was there but two boys who were quizzing each other. She hurried over to the reference section and found the volume she wanted. Then she took it to a table by the window.

A thick yellow paperback, *The Farmer's Almanac* was a book of information on hundreds of topics. The book gave the exact dates for the phases of the moon and the time each would appear in different parts of the country. Curious, Tracy looked up the moon information for the day Stacy had disappeared, two weeks ago.

When she found the answer, her heart thudded heavily. Two weeks ago had been the day of the full moon. She didn't know exactly what time Stacy had gone through the mirror, but it was around nine at night. According to the almanac, the full moon had occurred at 9:08 P.M. that evening.

So that's the answer, Tracy thought. *The mirror opens up as a door to the past at the moment the full moon appears.* Excited, she skimmed through the book to find the next full moon, and was disappointed that it was two weeks away.

I'll never be able to keep fooling people that long, she realized. And even worse, could Stacy hold on that long? The last couple of times she'd seen her, her sister seemed to be frightened.

Tracy felt so frustrated she wanted to cry, but then she remembered that the carving of the new moon was as big as the one of the full moon. *Maybe the mirror works during the new moon too,* she thought.

The moon had been so dim the last few days that she knew the new moon must be coming up soon. She turned back in the almanac, and saw that the next new moon would occur on Sunday night at exactly eight-thirty! Then she realized—*today is Sunday!*

Tonight, she thought excitedly. *I'll be able to help Stacy get back tonight!*

She couldn't help grinning as she put the book back on the reference shelf. *The nightmare is almost over,* she kept thinking. *In just a few hours I'll have my sister back. I can stop pretending.*

All she had to do, in fact, was get through today. She planned to go to her room and stay there until it was time to bring Stacy home through the mirror.

Still smiling, Tracy gathered up her books and started out of the library. She was nearly at the door when a familiar voice stopped her.

"Excuse me."

She turned around to find Angela, who was library monitor for the day.

"Where are you going, *Stacy?*" she asked.

"Well, I just—" Tracy started to say, but Angela cut her off.

"Or should I say Tracy?" Angela went on. "Maybe you can fool everyone else, but you can't fool me. I finally figured out what's going on."

CHAPTER 16

STACY

IT'S tonight, Stacy kept thinking all day Sunday. *Tonight I'll escape back to my own world, my own time. All I have to do is wait.* She didn't know exactly what time the new moon would be, but Philomena had told her it would be after dinner.

She and Philomena spent most of the morning weeding the garden and cleaning the animal pens. It was hard work, but she'd been working so hard for so many days that she hardly noticed. She wondered if Philomena was thinking about that night too. *Probably not,* she decided. After all, Philomena thought she only wanted to look into the mirror. She would be in for a big surprise.

"Why so quiet, Stacy?" Philomena asked as they carried water buckets to the pigs.

"Oh, I'm just thinking of something," she said vaguely.

"Of your home?" Philomena said, smiling. "I understand how much you want to see it. And I promise, tonight you shall see your home one last time."

"Thank you, Philomena," said Stacy.

"It is my pleasure," Philomena said. "For I want you to be happy here—here where you will stay."

Stacy was trying to think how to answer when Granny Johnson's voice rang across the yard. "Philomena!" she called. "Get in here right now. I need your help!"

"Excuse me," Philomena said. "Can you water the hogs by yourself?"

"I think so," Stacy answered.

Philomena set down her water bucket and crossed the yard to the house. Stacy unlatched and opened the gate to the hog pen. Several of the piglets had been playing near the gate, and one of them suddenly darted out into the yard.

"Stop!" Stacy called. She knew that Granny Johnson would be furious if she let the pig get away, so she closed the gate and started chasing the pig. It seemed to think it was playing a game, and led her in circles to the back of the farmhouse and then into the woods.

"Come back here!" she shouted. If the pig got far into the forest, she'd never find it. She ran into the trees, darting after the pig as it zigzagged through the thick brush. Soon they were out of sight of the farmhouse, and Stacy began to worry about getting lost. "*Please* come back!" she called after the pig.

A little farther on the pig stopped in a clearing and

began to munch on some yellow flowers. Stacy sneaked up and scooped the tiny animal up in her arms. "Gotcha!" she said. She was about to start back when a movement caught her eye. Curious, she walked to the edge of the clearing, and could hardly believe what she saw.

Fluttering in the light breeze were three white cloth banners, each tied to a crude cross made of sticks. The crosses were stuck upright in mounds of loose earth, mounds that looked like graves.

Stacy reached out and unrolled one of the banners, then dropped it immediately in horror. Written on the banner, and on each of the other two, was the crudely lettered word: SISTER.

CHAPTER 17

TRACY

"**W**ELL, Tracy?" Angela said, smiling triumphantly "Or should I call you Stacy? Or does it matter?"

"I—I don't know what you're talking about," Tracy said, her heart pounding.

"Oh, don't you?" said Angela. "Well, I think you do. And I think you'd better tell me before I tell everyone else what's going on."

"Tell you what?" Tracy asked.

"Tell me why you're pretending to be Stacy!" Angela said. "You might fool everyone else, but you can't fool me. I know you're really Tracy!"

Desperately, Tracy tried to think of a way to escape. She couldn't, so she met Angela head on. "What makes you think that?" she whispered to her sister's friend.

Angela smiled again. "Come on, Tracy," she said. "I know Stacy really well, and even if you did fool me last week, I know you're not her. You've been covering for each other for days. At first I thought it was just a joke. But now I know it's more. So tell me what's going on."

Tracy didn't say anything. She couldn't. She knew she couldn't fool Angela anymore. But somehow, she had to calm her down. She had to make her promise not to say anything until the next day, when Stacy would be back from the mirror—she hoped!

"All right," Tracy said at last. "You're right. We *have* been covering for each other."

"I knew it!" said Angela.

"But it's not what you think," Tracy went on, thinking fast.

"Then what is it? Why are you doing it?" Angela asked.

"It's because of my grades."

"Your grades?" Angela asked.

"Yes," Tracy said. "You see, you were right the other day. Stacy and I did have an argument."

"I knew it!" Angela exclaimed, a satisfied grin on her face. "What was it about?"

"Well"—Tracy stopped to think—"Stacy was annoyed that I wasn't studying enough."

"What's the big deal about that?" Angela asked.

"Mrs. Danita cut my town privileges till my grades come up," admitted Tracy.

"Really?" Angela said. "I didn't think they were *that* bad."

"Anyway, we have plans to visit our aunt Louise next week in Silverbell. If I don't get better grades, I can't go," Tracy explained. "So Stacy and I devised a plan that would give me more time to study."

"How?" asked Angela.

Tracy could feel her palms getting sweaty. "By having Stacy cover for me during the day, I could have more time to study in our room and in the library."

Angela stared suspiciously at Tracy. Tracy hoped that she believed her story.

Finally Angela said, "Okay, but you know you could have told me about this before. I wouldn't have told Mrs. Danita."

"Thanks, Angela," said Tracy, with apparent relief. "Now that I've told you the truth, please don't tell anyone else."

"I won't tell anyone for *now*," Angela said. "But tell Stacy—next time you talk to her—that I'll believe your crazy story if she tells me herself."

"Okay," Tracy agreed.

"That means," Angela went on, "that Stacy had better show up tonight for the History Honor Society party. And I mean the *real* Stacy. . . ."

CHAPTER 18

STACY

THE little banners continued to flutter in the breeze, and Stacy took a step back in horror.

The banners all said SISTER. But Philomena had only had one sister, Melody. Who, then, did these three graves belong to? Could these be the final resting places of the "others," the runaways Granny had spoken of?

The idea was too terrible to think about. But who else could be in the graves? And if it was the "others," how did they die? Stacy thought of the bloodstained axe in Philomena's closet and shuddered. *No,* she thought. *No, it can't be.* But she knew, deep in her heart, who had lettered the little banners. Philomena.

She felt as if a giant fist were squeezing her chest so she couldn't breathe. How could this be happening to her? *Tonight,* she told herself. *I'll get away tonight.*

The piglet had begun to squirm in her arms, so Stacy

turned and made her way back through the clearing to the pen. She put the little pig back inside, then began to water the animals, her head reeling with what she had seen.

"Stacy!"

She jumped at Philomena's voice.

"Are you all right?"

Stacy turned to see Philomena behind her.

"I've been calling you in to lunch," she went on. "Where have you been?"

Stacy explained about chasing the little pig into the forest. "I never knew they could run so fast," she added.

"Oh, yes, they can be quite a handful of trouble," Philomena said. "But is that all? You look so upset, sister Stacy."

"I guess I'm just tired," Stacy said, trying to hide her feelings. "It's hot today."

"Yes, and I know you aren't as accustomed to hard work as I am," Philomena said. "But I promise you that I will always help you. We will be like the truest of sisters to each other."

Sisters. At the word, Stacy couldn't help shuddering.

"Come along now," Philomena went on, taking Stacy's hand. Scarcely watching where she was walking, Stacy let Philomena lead her to the farmhouse door. *Tonight,* she kept thinking. *I'll get away tonight. All I have to do is remember that, to get through the rest of the day.*

Stacy followed Philomena into the kitchen, where

Granny Johnson was already eating her tasteless meal of salt pork and biscuits. Stacy was about to sit down at the table when she noticed there was something odd about the kitchen, something different.

All at once she saw it, and suddenly dizzy, Stacy wanted to faint. This couldn't be happening to her!

The mirror was gone.

Stacy just stared at the empty place along the wall where the mirror had stood.

No, she thought. *It can't be gone. It can't be!*

She turned and looked at Philomena and the old woman. Granny Johnson's face was impassive as she ate her lunch. Philomena was gazing directly at Stacy with a small smile.

How could they do this? she wondered. Her mouth was so dry she could hardly speak. "Where is the mirror?" she finally managed to ask.

"I sold it this morning," Granny Johnson said.

Stacy was so shocked she thought she must have heard wrong. "You *sold* it?"

"I only kept the mirror for Philomena, but this morning she told me she had no use for it. And I got a very fair price for it," the old woman said. "Besides, mirrors serve nothing but vanity. Far better to do your chores and keep to yourself."

"Come on, Stacy," urged Philomena. "Come sit and eat your lunch."

Mechanically, Stacy walked over to the table and sat. She watched as Philomena filled a plate for her, but made no move to eat. All she could think of was that because of Philomena, the mirror was gone, and with it all her hopes of returning to her own life were gone too.

"Who bought the mirror?" she asked, certain that Granny Johnson wouldn't answer her.

" 'Twas one of our neighbors," Granny replied, to Stacy's surprise. "Mr. Bendigo across the gully. He's admired the mirror in the past."

A neighbor bought it! Stacy thought with sudden hope. *That means it isn't far away.*

"He bought the mirror for his daughter's wedding, didn't he, Granny?" Philomena said.

"That's right," the old woman said. "The girl's to be married in San Francisco. The mirror is already on its way there by stagecoach."

For the rest of the day, Stacy felt as if she were sleepwalking. She did her chores without any memory of what she had just done. All that she could think about was the mirror, her only hope of escape. And now, thanks to Philomena, that hope was on the way to San Francisco, completely out of reach.

I can never go home, she thought again and again. *I have to stay here forever. I'll never see my room again, my friends, my sister.*

Then she remembered the three small graves. What if Philomena planned to kill her next?

"Don't be sad, dear Stacy," Philomena said. "You look so tired. Let me help you lift that bucket."

No wonder she's so cheerful, Stacy thought. She knows that I have to stay here with her forever.

Dinner that evening was a special treat—roasted chicken—but Stacy could scarcely taste it. All she wanted to do was get away from Philomena and her grandmother, even for a few minutes. She excused herself soon after eating, saying she wanted to check on the hogs.

"Very well," the old woman said. "But don't stay out too late. The woods are dangerous after dark."

"Yes," Stacy said mechanically. She crossed the yard to the hog pen, then circled it and walked into the woods, to the little clearing she had found that afternoon. She realized, as she was standing there, that it was just a few feet from what would be the soccer field at the Chilleen Academy, 140 years in the future. An early-evening breeze caused the banners on the crosses to flap back and forth like the wings of trapped birds.

Stacy stared at the three graves for a few moments, then felt the tears well up inside her and overflow. She sank down on her knees, buried her face in her hands and began to sob. "Oh, Tracy," she said softly. "Will I ever see you again?"

She cried until she had no more tears, then wiped her face on her handkerchief and stared again at the graves. The crying had helped, and she felt better, more clear-headed. *You're letting Philomena win*, she thought suddenly, and realized it was true. By refusing to fight or to think of an alternative, she was just giving up, abandoning herself to her fate.

She thought again of the bloody axe she had found in Philomena's room.

Could Philomena really have killed the girls?

With revulsion, Stacy shook her head. She didn't want to believe that Philomena could have done anything so terrible, but she remembered again the rage that distorted Philomena's face whenever Stacy talked about leaving. Maybe the other girls had tried to escape. Maybe Philomena hadn't been able to control herself. . . .

I've got to do something, she thought. *And I've got to do it fast.*

Granny Johnson had said Mr. Bendigo, the man who bought the mirror, lived "across the gully." She didn't know where that was, but somehow she would find it.

Stacy stood up, feeling better than she had in days. At last she knew what she had to do. She would find Mr. Bendigo and ask him where the mirror was. Maybe he hadn't shipped it yet. Maybe it was waiting in a shipping office somewhere. In any case, she would find it. If she had to, she'd follow it all the way to San Francisco.

The sunset had deepened and the sky was now indigo, with stars just beginning to appear. As she walked, she planned what she'd do. She already knew from a dozen landmarks that Granny Johnson's farmhouse was roughly where the barn at the Chilleen

Academy would someday stand. Maybe the "gully" was the deep, rocky streambed that the kids at Chilleen liked to hike along. It lay in the woods in the direction of Canyon Ridge, and she was sure she could find it. When she did, Mr. Bendigo's ranch had to be close by.

How far was it exactly? Would she be able to find it in the dark? Would she even reach it in time? More importantly, would she be able to sneak away without Philomena finding out?

CHAPTER 19

TRACY

THE History Honor Society party was scheduled to start at six-thirty in the dayroom. Tracy kept trying to think of a way to get out of going, but knew she couldn't.

It had begun to rain, and fierce thunder rattled the dormer windows of her room. *Too bad we aren't having the party outside,* she thought, *Then we could cancel it.*

Instead, she was going to have to play along with Angela and somehow convince everyone that she, Tracy, was really Stacy. She spent a longer time than usual getting ready for the party. She finally decided to wear a green-striped turtleneck sweater that was a favorite of Stacy's. She combed her hair down, fastening it with a green barrette. Critically, she studied herself in the mirror. *I do look exactly like Stacy now,* she thought.

Then she thought of the real Stacy. *I wonder what she's doing right now? Is she getting ready to come through the mirror in a couple of hours?*

She picked up a box of cookies she'd bought at the school store, took a deep breath, and started over to the dayroom, which was downstairs on the far side of the main building. She could tell from the noise that everyone was already there, eating snacks and listening to music. She greeted Stacy's friends as she entered, trying to act relaxed and normal.

"Hi, Stacy," Jimmy Tolliver said, his mouth full of potato chips.

"Hi, Jimmy," she said. "Hi, Dorie. Hi, Mrs. Douglas." She wondered where Angela was, and then a hand grabbed her arm and spun her around.

"Hello, Stacy," said Angela, suspicion in her eyes. "You are Stacy, aren't you?"

"Of course," said Tracy, forcing a little laugh.

"Well, I'm glad you showed up," Angela said with a smile.

"Thanks," Tracy answered. With a sigh of relief, she joined the other kids, and even managed to get into the spirit of the party, dancing and stuffing herself on junk food.

At 7:30 Tracy decided she had managed to fool Angela, mainly by staying out of her way and talking to other members of the club. *Just one more hour,* she thought, *and I'll never have to do this again.*

"May I have your attention, please," said Mrs. Douglas, who was standing by the door. "I'm very pleased you're all having such a good time. Now we're going to play history Jeopardy. The prize is a framed map of Phantom Valley from the last century."

She held up the map and the kids studied it curiously. The valley had far fewer people than now; Silverbell was just a speck in one corner. *I wonder where on that map Stacy has been living?* Tracy wondered.

"The way to win the map is to get the most points," Mrs. Douglas explained. "Mr. Taylor and I made up the questions. I've asked Dorie to keep score."

Uh-oh, Tracy knew that her sister Stacy would do really well at the game. But history was Tracy's worst subject, and everyone knew it.

"Would you like to go first, Stacy?" Mrs. Douglas asked, as if reading her thoughts.

"I don't know," said Tracy, her heart pounding violently. Mrs. Douglas was Stacy's favorite teacher, and Tracy didn't want to do anything to make her suspicious. "I'm pretty tired tonight," she went on. "Maybe someone else should go?"

"Don't be shy," Mrs. Douglas said. "After all, you're one of our best students in history. Surely you're not worried about a little game?"

"I guess not," Tracy said. "Go ahead."

Mrs. Douglas smiled encouragingly and read off the first question on the list. "The answer," she said, "is 'The first ten amendments to the Constitution.' "

The first ten what? For just a moment Tracy panicked. Then she remembered that she'd just been reading about the Constitution while studying for Stacy's midterm. *Don't panic*, she told herself. *Think*. Then she had it. "The Bill of Rights," she said. Quickly, she remembered to rephrase it in the form of a question. "What is the Bill of Rights?"

Mrs. Douglas smiled and nodded. "Very good, Stacy," she said. "Jimmy? You're next."

The game went on and on, with the questions getting harder each round. Tracy wasn't able to answer all the questions, but to her surprise, she did well enough to still be in the game half an hour later.

Will this game ever end? she wondered. It was already a little after eight. She had to get back to her room. She got up from the sofa where she'd been sitting. "Hey, guys," she said, "I'm sorry, but I'm really tired. Great party, Angela."

"Oh, dear," Mrs. Douglas said. "Can't you stay a few more minutes? You're tied for the lead."

Again Tracy remembered how much Stacy liked Mrs. Douglas. "Okay, a few more minutes," she said, sitting back down.

Ten minutes later the only contestants remaining were "Stacy" and Jimmy Tolliver. Tracy could hardly believe that she had done so well. The final question, about the French and Indian War, was so hard that she doubted even the real Stacy could have answered it. Her answer was wrong, but Jimmy couldn't answer it either, so the game was declared a tie.

"I know it's late," Mrs. Douglas said after congratulating the two winners, "but we need to plan our next meeting."

"I'm sorry," said Tracy. "I really have to get back to my room."

"Please don't leave yet," Mrs. Douglas said. "Not now. Your input is very important to the club."

Tracy looked at her watch. It was 8:15. "Well, I guess a few more minutes won't hurt," she said. She scarcely listened while the other kids talked about an upcoming field trip. *I've got to get out of here,* she thought. It was 8:25 when Mrs. Douglas at last shut her planning book.

"Well," she said. "That's all the official business for now. I look forward to seeing you all at our next meeting."

Tracy was already on her feet and at the door when Mrs. Douglas's voice stopped her. "Stacy, dear?"

Tracy looked at her watch. It was 8:26.

"Do you have a minute?" Mrs. Douglas said. "I have to talk to you about something very important."

"Well I—" Tracy started to say.

"I promise this won't take long," Mrs. Douglas went on, taking Tracy's hand. "Now, I won't take no for an answer."

CHAPTER 20

STACY

STACY waited impatiently for Granny Johnson and Philomena to go to bed. As soon as Philomena was asleep, Stacy untied the key from around Philomena's neck and unlocked the bedroom door. Granny Johnson had thrown Stacy's jeans and T-shirt into the rag pile that she kept by her sewing box. Quickly Stacy changed into her own clothes and crept out of the house into the still, black night.

The only illumination was from the stars, and Stacy looked at the looming woods with a growing feeling of unease. She remembered that Granny Johnson had said the woods could be dangerous at night. In her own time the forest in Phantom Valley was said to be haunted.

Stop scaring yourself! she told herself sternly. *It's just pine woods. You've walked in the woods a million times. Besides, it's the only way to find the mirror and get back home.*

Once she was inside the trees, it was even darker. She couldn't see more than a few inches in front of her. All around she could hear the sounds of the night: the chirping of insects, the rustling of small animals, the cries of night-hunting birds. She remembered reading that wolves and bears had been common in Phantom Valley in the last century, and she felt a little shiver go down her spine.

Just concentrate on walking, she told herself. *Just put one foot in front of another. It can't be far.*

Soon she settled into a rhythm of walking, still alert but concentrating on moving as quickly as possible. The loudest sound now was her own footsteps on the dry pine needles.

Crunch.

Stacy jumped at the sudden sound close behind her. It could be a footstep. The footstep of something big and heavy. She stopped, listening carefully, but the sound wasn't repeated. It must have been a pinecone falling from a tree, she decided.

She continued to walk, more quickly now. She was beginning to wonder if she'd been going in the right direction. Mr. Bendigo lived beyond the gully, but where?

Crunch. Crunch.

She whirled, checking behind her, but all she could see was inky darkness. Was something following her? She began to run, ignoring the branches that scratched her face, the rocks that threatened to trip her.

Where was the gully? Had she been going in circles?

Suddenly she pitched forward and rolled down a steep embankment. When she reached the bottom she waited a moment for her heart to stop pounding, then picked herself up, almost crying with relief. She had finally come to the gully, the large streambed that ran through the forest. Mr. Bendigo's ranch should be just on the other side.

Her right arm was a little stiff because she had fallen on it, but she wasn't really hurt. Carefully, she picked her way up the far, sloping side and hurried on through the forest. In a few moments she reached a large clearing. In the starlight, she could see, just ahead of her, the dark outline of Mr. Bendigo's ranch house. A little to one side stood a large barn.

I've made it, she thought. *I'm here.*

Crunch.

She must have imagined it. The crunching noise began again, and then it was repeated, in a regular rhythm. *Crunch, crunch, crunch.* Whatever it was, it had to be big. *A bear,* she thought in panic. *Or a wolf.*

She imagined the sharp claws and fangs, the animal's hot breath as it closed in for the kill.

"No!" she cried.

She ran toward the ranch house, but all the windows were dark. What could she do? Should she pound on the door, ask for help? What if Mr. Bendigo refused to help her? What if he didn't even hear her?

Stacy glanced over her shoulder, saw the black shape of something coming toward her, fast. The barn was right ahead of her, its door slightly ajar. She ran through the small opening, then slammed it behind her.

Safe. She was safe for now. But would she be able to find the—

Then she saw it. The mirror, standing against a large wooden crate. She thought she had never seen anything so beautiful in her life.

She ran toward it, her heart pounding excitedly. The glass looked like an inky pool of water in the faint light. Would she be able to see the images from her home? With trembling hands she reached out and pressed the carvings of the new and full moons.

At first nothing happened. She pressed them again. Then, as she watched, her old room began to appear in the depths of the mirror. It became brighter and brighter, until she felt she could touch it.

Where was Tracy?

She reached forward, about to touch the mirror, when a noise behind her made her turn.

In the light coming from the mirror she could clearly see the barn door. It was slowly opening. Silhouetted against the dark sky was an even darker figure, and in its hand was an axe.

CHAPTER 21

TRACY

GASPING for breath, Tracy ran down the hall toward her wing. Time was ticking away. She had to hurry. She reached the stairs for the wing that led up to her room. Without pausing, she ran up the stairs two at a time.

She had managed to escape from Mrs. Douglas by telling her politely, but firmly, that she would see her Monday morning. Then she left before the teacher could say anything else.

As it was, she had less than two minutes to get to the mirror. What would happen if she were late? How long would the "window" to the past remain open?

I'm coming, Stacy, she thought. *I'm coming.*

Without slowing down, she pushed her door open and rushed to the mirror.

This is it, she thought. *This is my chance to bring Stacy back.*

The mirror reflected only her room.

In growing panic Tracy checked her watch. It was exactly eight-thirty. *Maybe the moon couldn't activate the mirror because of all the clouds*, she thought. As she glanced out the window, she could see stars beginning to sparkle in the inky night sky.

Looking back at the mirror again, she began to see images appear. Instead of the old-fashioned kitchen, the mirror filled with the interior of some large, dark place. In the background she could just make out thick wooden beams hung with ropes. What was this place? More important, where was the kitchen? Where was Stacy?

Panicking, Tracy ran her hands over the carvings at the top of the mirror, but nothing changed. Had the new moon caused the mirror to open into another world entirely? Had she lost her contact with the old-fashioned kitchen and Stacy?

She continued to peer into the mirror, frantic. Then she saw movement, and Stacy's face appeared.

"Stacy!" she cried, overwhelmed with relief.

At the same moment that Tracy spoke, Stacy's face lit up with recognition for an instant. There was something wrong, though. Tracy could see that her sister was badly frightened.

"Don't worry, Stacy," she said, even though she knew her twin couldn't hear. "I'm going to bring you home now."

Slowly and confidently she reached toward the mirror. As her fingertips touched the glass surface, she felt a strange tingling, almost like an electric shock, and then her hands passed through the glass, into the world of the mirror.

From the other side Stacy was reaching toward her twin. Now the girls' fingers touched, and they clasped hands. Tracy made sure she had a good grip, then began to pull, gently tugging her sister to her side of the mirror.

She could feel Stacy moving toward her, but then, suddenly, Stacy's body jerked. Instead of pulling Stacy through to her own world, Tracy felt *herself* being pulled—into the mirror!

CHAPTER 22

STACY/TRACY

STACY felt an electric tingle as her fingers touched the mirror. In a second she was holding Tracy's warm hands in hers.

Then, a moment later, something grabbed her by the shoulders, hard.

Without turning around, Stacy knew it was Philomena. She tried to twist and pull away, to go into the mirror with Tracy, but it was no use.

With superhuman strength Philomena was pulling Stacy back, pulling both twins back, through the mirror and into the world of the past.

Without letting go of her sister's hands, Stacy turned her head to confront Philomena. Before she could do or say anything, Stacy felt something hit her, hard, on the head. The mirror and the barn swirled dizzily before her. Then everything went black.

★　★　★

"No!" Tracy cried, her heart hammering. "Let us go!" She struggled, trying to pull her sister back out of the mirror. She yanked as hard as she could, but still felt herself being drawn through the mirror, drawn to the other side. Her body tingled as it passed through the glass, half in, half out. Tracy blinked, trying to see in the darkness. Her nostrils filled with a familiar, musty odor, and she realized the dark place was a barn.

With a sudden lurch, Stacy fell to the floor and lay there, unmoving. "Stacy!" Tracy called. "Stacy!" Her sister's eyes were closed, and Tracy saw an ugly red welt on her forehead that hadn't been there before. What had happened to her? For one heart-stopping moment Tracy wondered if her sister were dead. No, Stacy's hands were warm. With all her strength, Tracy held on to them. She was still half in the mirror and half out of it.

I've got to keep contact with my own world, she thought. She hooked her feet around the bottom of the mirror frame in her room, then shifted her grip so that she was holding Stacy's wrists.

"I'm going to bring you home now, Stacy," she said to her unconscious sister. "Help me if you can." To Tracy's relief, Stacy's eyes fluttered open. Tracy started to pull upward, but Stacy hardly moved. She was too weak to help. At the same time, Tracy felt herself being drawn farther into the world of the mirror by her sister's weight. "Help me!" she cried again, but she knew from Stacy's terrified expression that her sister could do nothing more.

Tracy fought to keep her feet hooked around the bottom of the mirror, but suddenly felt her right foot being jerked loose.

No, she thought. *No, I've got to hold on or we'll both be trapped in the mirror world.*

Something moved in the darkness behind Stacy. Before she could make it out, Stacy had turned her head and was screaming in terror.

Standing above Stacy was the red-haired girl Tracy had first seen in the old-fashioned kitchen. The girl was pale beneath her freckles, and her expression was mad.

She's the one, Tracy thought. *She's the one who's trying to pull me through the mirror. She knocked Stacy on the head, and now she won't let me bring Stacy home.*

Horrified, Tracy watched as the girl slowly raised her arms. In her hands was a heavy axe with dark stains on its blade. She raised the axe above her head and held it there a moment as she looked first at Tracy, then at Stacy. Her face twisted in a hideous smile, and then she whispered a single word: "Sister."

CHAPTER 23

STACY/TRACY

FOR a moment there was utter silence, and then Stacy began to scream again. The red-haired girl was swinging the axe down, straight at Stacy.

"No!" Tracy screamed. With more strength than she knew she had, she pulled her sister out of the way. As she did, she lifted one foot and it came away from its anchor at the bottom of the mirror.

Thunk! The axe blade bit into the dirt floor of the barn.

While Tracy struggled to rehook her foot under the mirror frame again, the red-haired girl pulled the axe out of the ground and brought it up over her head.

She's going to kill us both! Tracy thought wildly. *She's going to chop us into pieces!* "Help me, Stacy!" she begged again.

She got her foot secured under the mirror just as the girl was ready to swing her arms down again. Stacy stirred, her eyes opening wide.

115

"Now!" Tracy cried, and she yanked, lifting Stacy off the floor, lifting her into the mirror.

Tracy felt the strange tingling as her body moved from the world of the past back into the world of the present. With a final tug, she pulled Stacy all the way through, and the twins fell to the floor, the floor of their room at Chilleen.

A second later there was a hideous screeching sound. Tracy raised her eyes to the mirror and saw a horrifying sight: slicing through the mirror, from top to bottom, was an axe blade. Almost as if in slow motion, the mirror was cut in two, then fell to the floor, where the glass shattered into hundreds of tiny pieces.

Tracy loosened her hold on her sister's wrists and slid her fingers up to grip her sister's hands. Nothing remained of the mirror but splinters of wood and glass. There was no sign of the axe, no sign of the red-haired girl.

"You're safe now, Stacy," she murmured to her sister.

Epilogue

"I'M so glad you girls could come today," Aunt Louise said, setting a chocolate mousse in the center of the table. "I've been dying for you to see my apartment."

"It looks great, Aunt Louise," said Tracy.

"You've got so many nice things here," agreed Stacy.

"I was so sorry to hear about the accident that happened to your mirror," Aunt Louise said.

"It was the strangest thing," Tracy said. "It just fell over one night."

"You never know with old things," Louise said. "But don't worry about it. I've been looking around and I'm going to try to replace it."

"Actually," Stacy said, looking at her sister, "we found out we didn't really need a mirror. Maybe a framed picture would be better."

"Whatever you say," her aunt answered. "But I do want to get something—to celebrate the good midterm grades you both received."

"Isn't it great?" Stacy said. "Who would have thought Tracy's grades would end up nearly as good as mine?"

"I guess I've just learned how to study," said Tracy.

"Well, I'm very proud of both of you," Aunt Louise said. She turned her head at a knock on the door.

"That must be Angela," Stacy said. "We told her to meet us here for the bus ride back to Chilleen."

"Good," said Aunt Louise. "I've been wanting to meet some of your friends." She went to the door and introduced herself to Angela, then invited her in for dessert.

"Terrific," Angela told her. "Chocolate's my favorite flavor." She greeted the twins, then laughed. "What are you two up to?" she said. "How come you dressed alike today?"

"I talked the girls into it," Aunt Louise said, cutting into the mousse. "I wanted to take pictures to send to the family back east."

"You know something, Stacy?" Angela said. "If you guys dressed like this all the time, you'd have everyone in school confused."

"What about you?" the twin said. "Wouldn't you be confused too?"

Angela laughed. "Me?" she said. "Of course not. You know I've always been able to tell the two of you apart."

"Is that so?"

"Of course, Stacy," she said. "I can tell you from

Tracy any time. There's something about your voice, and the color of your hair. . . ."

"Really?" answered the twin. "Well, I guess we won't even try to fool you. Isn't that right, *Tracy?*" she added, winking at her sister.

Stacy, who hadn't said a word since Angela entered, started laughing. "Right," she said. "Against someone like Angela, we wouldn't have a chance!"

About the Author

LYNN BEACH was born in El Paso, Texas, and grew up in Tucson, Arizona. She is the author of many fiction and nonfiction books for adults and children.

Coming next—

Phantom Valley ™

THE SPELL

(Coming in June 1992)

Mikki Merrill is assigned to read to a colorful, somewhat bizarre, elderly woman for her work-study project. Slowly the woman's special powers are revealed—she is able to cast spells on people! Mikki knows she shouldn't mess around with magic, but she has to get back at her roommate Diane. She is just too beautiful, too snobby, too mean. What better way than with a little magic? So with the help of the old woman, Mikki casts a spell. Mikki soon finds out the hard way, though, that there is no such thing as a *little* magic—and now she's the one in great danger!